A Lively Companion

An Austen Ensemble, Book 1

Corrie Garrett

Kindle Direct Publishing
LOS ANGELES, CALIFORNIA

Corrie Garrett
28 Amherst Rd.
Morgantown, WV 26505
www.corriegarrett.com

Publisher's Note: This is a work of fiction. Names, characters, places, and incidents are a product of the author's imagination. Locales and public names are sometimes used for atmospheric purposes. Any resemblance to actual people, living or dead, or to businesses, companies, events, institutions, or locales is completely coincidental.

Book Layout ©2017 BookDesignTemplates.com

A Lively Companion/ Corrie Garrett. -- 1st ed.
ISBN 978-1-6763734-4-5

Dedicated to my dear husband who did not cause me nearly so much drama as poor Mr. Darcy and Lizzy, but proposed before sunrise on Christmas morning so that we could have our misty, romantic walk before my loud family intervened.

"There is a stubbornness about me that never can bear to be frightened at the will of others. My courage always rises at every attempt to intimidate me."

–JANE AUSTEN, PRIDE AND PREJUDICE

L IZZY READ HER FATHER'S LETTER with consternation. She hovered by the fence post, one foot on the stile, arrested in mid-step. The fine cream paper covered with her father's bold writing quivered in the morning breeze.

He "strongly encouraged" her to accept Lady Catherine's offer? Despite the loss of her company being his "daily sacrifice," and even the "unpleasantness" she might endure?

Lizzy raised her eyes blindly to the misty grass of the field, then over her shoulder to the tall, bare tree line at the edge of Rosings Park. A gardener used a scythe on the hedge below the trees; the faint *switch switch switch* of his precise strokes reached her ears as he shaped the prickly bushes with geometric precision.

This was Lady Catherine's domain, and Lizzy had been looking forward to *leaving* it, not joining it!

The formal roses near the house grew in proper, elegant beds with blooms evenly dispersed, as if even nature had bent to Lady Catherine's autocratic will. The many windows of the house shone in the light of the early sun, and the vines that grew on the walls didn't dare cross the panes by as much as a hairsbreadth.

She gathered her skirts and stepped up the stile and down to the other side to return to the parsonage.

Still distracted by her letter, Lizzy stumbled a little and the cold, wet grass soaked her ankles. She mumbled unhappily and lifted her skirts, walking slowly as she finished her father's letter.

He had invested in a scheme with a friend in London. "Yes, Lizzy, you may judge me," he wrote. "I know better, and yet I let your mother's worries infect me. In short, I thought it might be worthwhile to grow the portion I will leave to you girls, which mismanagement has rendered rather less than it might have been. True change in our habits is apparently beyond me, or at least it cannot hold my attention long enough to enact it. Therefore I looked for an easy answer and received what such seekers generally do. To be blunt, I cannot even provide the thousand pounds you girls should be able to expect. Perhaps I speak more freely as this is a letter, but such it is. I am humiliated, but don't worry—such things are quickly dulled in the pages of Homer. Go to Tunbridge Wells. Meet new people, write me stories of Lady Catherine's eccentricities, and give me a few months to deal with my chagrin before I must face you. Please, Lizzy?"

Lizzy was shocked, yet also... not. Her father was sensible but had failed to implant much sense of economy in her mother. She would've thought he was too wise to speculate, but perhaps he was only too indolent. Was the situation as bad as he feared? Or was he overreacting to a loss? She did not know.

In the face of Lady Catherine's rude persistence in her offer, Lizzy had asserted that her father would never countenance his daughter's absence for months more. Particularly if her absence was in order to become a *paid companion*, however temporary it might be.

Now Lizzy was counseled to accept. He advised her to lower herself to become a member of Lady Catherine's household staff! How humbling!

Though now Lizzy was perhaps the one overreacting. To be a companion was not at all the same as a laundry maid, or even a ladies' maid. Frequently a companion was merely a friend or family member, unpaid, but the fact that Lady Catherine offered a salary somehow made it worse.

Lady Catherine would love to hear Lizzy admit she was wrong.

It was almost intolerable. Lizzy was tempted to ignore her father's letter. But... Lizzy was too fond of him to dismiss the first distasteful request he'd put to her in years.

What kind of daughter only obeyed her father when he was indulgent and affectionate?

Her father had never exerted his authority the way she sometimes wished, particularly with Lydia and Kitty. How hypocritical it would be to shrug off his one request?

Lizzy's shadow stretched in front of her as she walked westward, the rising sun warm on her back. When another shadow overtook hers, she was not surprised to look up and find Mr. Darcy catching up to her on the small path.

He often walked here, she'd found, and often with her, for lack of other companions.

"Miss Bennet," he greeted her.

"Mr. Darcy." He didn't seem to find conversation necessary, which was the only consolation of his presence.

"Your visit has gone too quickly."

Lizzy sighed. Why did he want to talk *today*? "On the contrary, I feel I've been gone from Longbourn quite a lengthy time."

"I misspoke. I should have said that your visit has gone too quickly for me, as has my own. But then I do not have a family at home missing me." He nodded to her letter.

Lizzy nodded quizzically. Her visit had been too short for *him*? What did that mean? Her visit had nothing to do with him.

"I believe you depart in two days?" he persisted.

"I had been planning to do so, but..." Lizzy paused. He hadn't been privy to his aunt's offer (made before he came), and Lizzy was reluctant to commit herself. But she already knew her decision, didn't she? She might as well embrace the humiliation.

"But," she repeated, more firmly, "Lady Catherine has asked me to be a temporary companion to Miss de Bourgh. You have probably heard that Mrs. Jenkinson is going away for a time. I believe I shall accept."

Mr. Darcy stopped. "A companion to Anne? You?"

Lizzy laughed, her ready sense of the ridiculous tickled. How absurd it must seem to Mr. Darcy, who disapproved of her and her family so completely! He probably thought Lady Catherine would do as well to hire an outright hoyden.

"Indeed. Lady Catherine is planning a trip to Tunbridge Wells to let Anne take the waters. Lady Catherine wishes her to have an... energetic companion."

She saw his lips involuntarily form the word *energetic*, as if trying to understand it. If she'd said Lady Catherine desired an ill-bred or vulgar companion, he could hardly have looked more confused.

"I daresay I shall be able to run many small errands for Miss de Bourgh, to the library for instance, while she recruits her strength," Elizabeth offered.

"But surely my aunt wouldn't—she would never—I beg your pardon, you surprised me. They would be fortunate to have you," Darcy corrected himself.

"Well, they are so fortunate," Lizzy said. "They will have me, though whether Lady Catherine will still desire my company after a fortnight, I wouldn't dare to guess."

Mr. Darcy smiled involuntarily, and Lizzy wondered again if a sense of humor lurked far (*far*) under his stoic demeanor. It was a pity he was such a prideful man.

True, he hadn't been so awful at Rosings, just silent. Lizzy didn't approve of silence in general, but it was even worse in a setting like Rosings where a real conversationalist was a treasure beyond words.

Mr. Darcy still looked perplexed.

"You are thinking it is unlike your aunt to willingly saddle herself with someone like me," Lizzy said. "You are quite right. But if you consider the vast amount of correction I need, I believe you will see the appeal."

Mr. Darcy only shook his head. "I don't believe you need correction."

"What?" Lizzy laughed in surprise at this unexpected gallantry. "Take care! I might mistake your politeness for flattery."

"You don't need her correction, at any rate," he amended.

"That is an admission, indeed. I suspect I shall have it nonetheless."

Darcy studied her face as she walked. He felt completely floored by this development.

"Why would you accept?" he finally asked. "Do you so desperately need—" He cut himself off. Unthinkable to question her need for money. Her father, though not wealthy, was certainly able to provide for his daughters. They needn't *hire themselves out*.

"Do you desire occupation?" he asked instead. He could well see that being confined to Meryton would grow tedious for her.

"I am always willing to try new things," Elizabeth said, without at all illuminating the matter.

Perhaps she did contemplate future employment. How dismal and how... unnecessary. Elizabeth had no large dowry, he suspected, but with her looks and intelligence, her sweetness and engaging manner, there was still every possibility of her achieving an eligible match. *Every* possibility.

Had she given up on marriage after the incident with Mr. Collins? The stupid man had been unable to stay silent on the matter of her rejection, as any man of common sense would have.

"Then you will be with my aunt for the foreseeable future," Darcy mused. It certainly gave him time to think. Elizabeth's coming departure had acted on him so strongly that he'd been on the point of throwing all his scruples to the wind and proposing.

But should he? There was no rush now, and he began to feel rather foolish for coming to the brink of a marriage proposal based on nothing more than an artificial deadline. He was not normally an impulsive man. He should be absolutely certain before he committed himself.

If Elizabeth wasn't returning to the wilds of Hertfordshire (and her untamed family), he had plenty of time to know his own mind.

Darcy realized belatedly that they'd almost reached the parsonage.

"I hope you'll enjoy your time with Anne," he said. "Please excuse me."

Darcy strode back to Rosings with a curiously light heart. As much as he didn't care for Lady Catherine's overbearing nature, she was undoubtedly well-bred, the pink of gentility. Perhaps it would be good for Elizabeth to travel about with her. Elizabeth's natural sweetness made her universally pleasing, but there could be no doubt that she'd lacked opportunities to gain experience among the gentry.

True, being a paid companion was generally considered low, but it might in this case be offset by the fact that Elizabeth was young and well-bred and had become known to them through mutual friends rather than application. Somehow those things became known. It was not as if she were hired as a governess or lady's maid, something truly menial.

His aunt would be dictatorial, it was her nature, but she would not treat Elizabeth like a servant. On the whole, he was quite pleased at this turn of events. It even made him think more pleasantly of Lady Catherine than he had for quite some time.

And when Lady Catherine asked him to accompany them to Tunbridge Wells while they got settled, he accepted.

His cousin, Colonel Fitzwilliam, abruptly swallowed a large bite of biscuit. "Were you not saying that you need to return to Pemberley next week?" he asked.

Lady Catherine answered for him. "I am sure he cannot begrudge us a few more days. Why should you seek to speed him away? It is very proper in him to lend us his protection."

"Very proper," Colonel Fitzwilliam echoed, with a raised eyebrow.

"Yes, well." Darcy was too honest with himself not to know exactly why he'd accepted, but he needn't share his heart with the whole neighborhood. "I have half a mind to find a new situation for Georgiana. She could do with a holiday as well."

"Didn't she have a long stay in Ramsgate last year?" Anne asked. "I wanted to go, but— "

"But you caught a putrid sore throat and were lucky it didn't turn to pneumonia," Lady Catherine cut in.

Darcy tensed at the mention of Ramsgate. Thankfully, no one except himself and Colonel Fitzwilliam knew about Georgiana's fiasco there. No one knew how George

Wickham had convinced his young sister to elope, convinced her that she was madly in love with him and vice versa.

Georgiana's heart had been bruised when she realized it was all greed and deceit, and her fragile pride had been crushed. Darcy was strongly hoping that the story would never be known.

Colonel Fitzwilliam smiled at Anne. "Tunbridge Wells? What a change for you, cousin. You feel well enough to travel?"

"I don't know, but— "

"But I have decided she would be better for the waters. Dr. Baillie says they do wonders for the unbalanced phlegmatic humors. I have asked Miss Elizabeth Bennet to accompany us. She has written to her father to get permission, and I expect it any day."

Anne looked up. "I was still hoping that Mrs. Collins might be prevailed upon to accompany us. Surely Mr. Collins could spare her for a few weeks."

"Nonsense. She has her duties here and should not spend her time attending you."

"As a friend—"

"No, Miss Elizabeth will do."

Colonel Fitzwilliam refrained from choking this time. He looked to Darcy. "Did I not see you walking with Miss Bennet this morning?"

"Yes. She did, in fact, receive a letter from her father. No doubt she will send a note of acceptance sometime today."

"Excellent," said Lady Catherine. "She has a decided, somewhat masterful way about her, but I hold that any fault except deceit can be trained out of a young woman of quality, with a proper mentor. She is not ideal, but she has a great deal of energy, and I believe will benefit from my tutelage and Anne's refined company."

Darcy grimaced. His aunt never sounded worse than when she was assuming fresh authority. Even more disquieting was that her words about Elizabeth's improvement in their society were unpleasantly close to his own earlier thoughts.

"What a wonderful notion," Colonel Fitzwilliam said, "to ask Miss Bennet to join you. A most pleasant young woman." He gave Darcy a significant look.

Darcy didn't say anything else and allowed his aunt to enumerate the advantages of the Wells. He could only hope his decision regarding Elizabeth would make itself plain in the coming weeks.

{ 2 }

*D*EAR *P*APA,

I have told Lady Catherine of your gracious consent to her charming scheme, and she is full of satisfaction. Whether her satisfaction is a worthy benchmark of right actions I must leave to your conscience.

Truly, Father, if you had seen her and my cousin Mr. Collins—the former expressing her own excellence in arranging the matter and the latter repeating it with such smiles and smirks!—oh, it was too much.

I know you have enjoyed my letters about them over the last weeks, but if I find that you have encouraged me to stay merely for the enjoyment of my descriptions, you will find me far less tractable in future.

No, I acquit you of indifference to my plight. I am sorry to hear of the bad investment, but I know far more gentlemen than you have been caught in such things. I cannot judge you, certainly, for I do not know what I would do in such a situation. Let us leave that.

I admit I am curious to visit Tunbridge Wells, and that there may be some benefit to cultivating my acquaintance with Lady Catherine. Whether I can further my acquaintance with Miss Anne de Bourgh is still a matter of some uncertainty, however. I frequently received more encouragement when conversing with my two goats. How are Periwinkle and Persephone? Have you seen them when you were at the farm, and have you assured yourself that the other goats are not making Persephone's life a misery? I did not know when I named her that she would be quite so forlorn and ready to be shunned by normal goatdom. She needs to find her Hades to give her life a little spice.

But I know you have done nothing of the sort, and indeed would not be able to distinguish them on sight, so I will not pester you.

If you care to pass on details to Mama, you may tell her that we leave for Tunbridge Wells in six days, and that we will be accompanied by Mr. Darcy and Colonel Fitzwilliam, whom I have spoken of previously. He is most gentlemanly, affable and talkative, and has made the many evenings spent in Lady Catherine's dining room bearable.

The Colonel is almost as talkative as Mr. Darcy is silent, and again I wonder at Mr. Darcy's ability to collect lively companions. You are a studier of human nature; what is his secret? Because this mystery is throwing my previous understanding awry. Bingley and the Colonel do not hang about him for his wealth, nor are they so loyal merely out of expediency. Even Colonel Fitzwilliam, who seems to be somewhat at his cousin's mercy, has nothing but praise to bestow! Would that I knew his secret, for heaven knows Lydia and Kitty, and even Mary, would never praise me to the skies.

You have nothing to fear, or to hope, from Colonel Fitzwilliam, by the by. He is a younger son of another of Mr. Darcy's aunts, and must, I believe, marry well. You would not ask this question, but Mama will, so I have provided the answer pre-inquiry.

I must go prepare for church. Mr. Collins has my undying gratitude, because he has made my future years of church-attendance a thing of anticipation. I will never criticize another homily by our good Mr. Wilson. After six weeks here, I now perceive that Mr. Wilson is a paragon of saintly virtues and needle-sharp theology.

Adieu,

Lizzy

Lizzy was not sorry, several hours later, to listen to the last of her cousin's lectures at church. Mr. Collins wasn't more severe than the average parson, but his sermons lacked all interest. They were completely derivative and may well have been quoted directly from Fordyce's sermons. She always struggled to respond honestly when he asked for her opinion, but she had finally realized she could at least praise his powers of memorization and recitation, which pleased him.

After the service, she waited in front of the church for Charlotte, enjoying the midmorning sun.

Mr. Collins stood in the vestibule to bid farewell to his parishioners. At least, that was his stated purpose; he'd instead monopolized Colonel Fitzwilliam and Mr. Darcy. They were trapped between him and the last pew, while the other congregants happily slipped out the door.

Charlotte stepped down onto the gravel path outside the church, bidding farewell to a plump woman with four or five sons orbiting about her with barely contained energy.

Charlotte tapped the shoulder of the littlest. "You did a fine job of listening today, Matthew. Much improved."

He grinned. "I know. Mama said I may have extra pudding if I didn't kick or whisper. And I did not."

The woman's face went red. "I didn't say—well, I know the parson says we oughtn't *bribe* the children—a good conscience is its own reward—"

Charlotte smiled quickly and broke off the poor woman's floundering. "I daresay a good conscience is improved with a healthy dose of pudding."

The woman lowered her voice. "Many do say a bribe will harden their hearts… but I admit it is sometimes helpful!"

Charlotte frowned. "I have no children of my own yet, so I certainly can't say... but your boys don't appear to have hard hearts. I think a reward for self-control is not wrong— it's a... a representation of the rewards of holy obedience. After all, we must believe that the good Lord 'rewards those who earnestly seek him.'"

Lizzy felt her eyes open wide. Her friend had never been much of a theologian, but apparently she'd given these things more thought in the last few months. Charlotte had always had excellent sense.

The woman repeated Charlotte's last phrase and smiled at her. "Well, that is what I have always thought, but never said so well!"

Charlotte nodded her head sensibly. "I hope you'll be willing to advise me when I have my own children."

The woman smiled proudly. "I've raised eight children. There's not much of 'em I haven't learned." She leaned in, a little conspiratorially. "If you do need any advice, while you're increasing, I hope you will let me know."

She headed on her way with a significant look, and Lizzy saw that Charlotte was looking flushed. Merciful heavens, *was* Charlotte expecting?

Miss de Bourgh also stood nearby, waiting for her mother who was still within the church. Charlotte turned to Miss de Bourgh, and they spoke quietly for several minutes.

The whole interchange had engrossed Lizzy. She hadn't really pictured what role Charlotte would play in her husband's social circle, but now that Lizzy saw it in action, it made perfect sense. Charlotte was so sensible, good-natured, and kind—of course the people would love her. She wouldn't undermine her husband directly, but she might *expand* on his dictates in her own way.

She had friends, Lizzy realized with relief, as another matron engaged Charlotte. Friends who perhaps valued Charlotte as much as Lizzy did, though in a different way. Charlotte's life was still unenviable to Lizzy, but perhaps with friends it would be bearable. And with children...! But with such a father!

Lizzy hadn't given much thought to her own potential children, feeling it unlikely that she would ever marry. She would certainly not relish her children's father being a stupid, pompous man. She thought fleetingly of Mr. Wickham and was not enamored of that image either. Surely he would be a kind, amusing father, but... *careless* was the word that came to mind, though perhaps that was unfair.

Mr. Darcy had broken away from Mr. Collins and joined her in the sun.

Lizzy impulsively asked him, "Did you ever struggle to sit quietly in church when you were a child? I cannot picture it."

"Not overly. My attention did wander, but my father emphasized self-control from a young age."

"What did your mind wander to?"

He smiled briefly, "Usually fishing, at that age. My father would sometimes take me at dawn before the service, when the fish were biting. What about you, Miss Elizabeth?"

She shook her head. "I must admit I often whispered with my sisters or made up stories about my neighbors which would cause me to laugh. I was always told to be more like Jane."

He nodded, but didn't reply, looking away uncomfortably. Lizzy narrowed her eyes. It had not been confirmed, but she still suspected that he'd helped to detach his friend Mr. Bingley from Jane. This was the most consciousness he'd shown yet.

"Jane was always the correct one," Lizzy continued. "She told me that she could not bear for the poor rector to look down and see *all* the children not attending. It would hurt his feelings, she was sure. She has always been the most considerate of us all."

"Indeed."

Charlotte and Colonel Fitzwilliam joined them, and Mr. Darcy immediately bowed and walked off with his cousin, who said a hasty goodbye.

Three days later, Lizzy devoted herself to packing. Charlotte shook out the dresses, while Lizzy carefully folded them the way Jane had taught her. Whom Jane had learnt it from, Lizzy wasn't sure, but Jane always seemed to absorb helpful habits like that.

Charlotte removed another dress from the armoire, vigorously shaking it. "I do hope you have a pleasant time. Miss de Bourgh is rather quiet and... and hard to know."

"You seem to know her. Does she not stop here nearly every time she rides out driving her ponies?"

"Yes. She is always particularly friendly with me; I do not know why." Charlotte looked a little self-conscious. "I do not mean to boast about it; I truly do not know why she stops to talk with me."

Lizzy knew what Charlotte's distinction meant, that she was not boasting about her friendship with the de Bourghs out of pride as her husband did. Lizzy waved her hand. "Of course not. I do not wonder at it. I always preferred you to the other young ladies of my acquaintance, and I had far more options than she. She is fortunate to have you as a friend."

"Still, I hope you will get along with her. And Lady Catherine can be..." She glanced toward the hall, where Mr. Collins was occasionally passing by. "She has a strong personality."

"Which is strongly understating the case," Lizzy agreed. "But you know how I delight in sketching the characters of those around me. And I would always pick the ridiculous, odd, or even wicked acquaintance over the dull.

Not that I mean to say Lady Catherine is any of those things."

"Certainly not dull," Charlotte agreed. "Nor is Mr. Darcy. You do not realize, since you haven't lived here nearly year-round like I have, but his behavior is most unusual. I was shocked to hear of him accompanying you to the Wells."

"He's not accompanying *me*. He's accompanying his aunt and cousin."

"He's never accompanied them anywhere before. I know you don't think it, but I hold to my opinion. I think you are keeping him here."

Lizzy folded the bodice of the muslin day dress and carefully rolled the skirt twice to avoid crushing and wrinkles.

"You must consider the possibility," Charlotte insisted. "He is a fine man, and if he should offer for you, I hope you would accept him."

Lizzy said nothing, pressing a paper over the dress. Did Charlotte still hold to her practical theory of marriage? *Still?* Lizzy felt too uncomfortable to even refer to Charlotte's decision all those months ago, and yet the conversation seemed to be veering that direction. She steered it away. "I can only say that if Mr. Darcy offers for me, I will write you immediately. Then you must come protect me. I suspect my life will be in danger if Lady Catherine believes I used her employment to such an end."

"You have an unexpected opportunity to know him better, and even build affection," Charlotte persisted. "I know that is paramount to you, and I won't try to argue you out of it. But if Mr. Darcy does improve on acquaintance, which Colonel Fitzwilliam has said, and you did feel affection..."

"I'd sooner feel affection for this new bonnet," Lizzy exclaimed. "It is also good-looking and although it occasionally gives me a sharp poke from this loose wire, at least it flatters my vanity."

Charlotte laughed. "You must marry a witty man, Lizzy, who will appreciate you. And if your children are half so sharp-tongued, you will have your just punishment."

Lizzy half-wanted to ask about what she'd overheard at church, as to whether Charlotte was expecting. But... she couldn't. Charlotte was so far out of her world now. Charlotte's decision was made, there was no drawing back. Could Charlotte be whole-heartedly glad to bring a baby into this house? *Should* she be?

To Lizzy's relief, Mr. Collins came over to make another of his congratulatory speeches and ended their tête-à-tête.

{ 3 }

M R. DARCY MOUNTED HIS HORSE and rode out ahead of the carriage with the Colonel, both allowing their horses to canter. Darcy's horse shifted fretfully under him and its hooves kicked up muck behind them.

When they reached it, the post road would offer a better surface for perhaps a quick gallop. The rain had left the lanes regrettably muddy.

Two blackbirds soared through the blue sky, and a light wind pulled at trees and waved the grasses in the ditch. It was a beautiful day for traveling, but he felt vaguely unsatisfied.

He would have enjoyed Elizabeth's company for the scant two hours it would take to reach Tunbridge Wells. If it had just been her, he would have chosen to ride inside the carriage, despite the glorious day.

But, of course, he would never have occasion to make a long carriage ride alone with her unless... unless he married her. As usual, that thought filled him with elation and guilt in equal measure.

Regardless, he would not have enjoyed Lady Catherine and Cousin Anne during this ride, so it was an easy choice to make. If he remembered correctly, driving long distances often rendered Anne queasy as well. He didn't envy Elizabeth's position.

In fact, he'd felt a bit defensive as he saw Elizabeth take the unenviable rear-facing seat without question. His aunt and cousin took the better bench, of course, but he longed to tell Elizabeth that she deserved preference over either of them. She'd cheerfully climbed up and remarked gaily just what he was thinking, that it was a beautiful day for traveling.

His aunt had immediately corrected her misapprehension, informing her that the east wind was particularly debilitating for Anne and that but for the reservation at the hotel, they would delay their journey. The carriage door shut before Darcy heard Elizabeth's reply, but he was left feeling unhappy.

In the carriage, Lizzy was not exactly wishing her life over, but if the hand of fate had suddenly plucked her out of the carriage she would not have complained. She thought she might even prefer Mr. Darcy's company to this solemn ride with Lady Catherine.

Anne leaned in the upholstered corner, wrapped in two shawls that nearly covered her bottle-green carriage dress. Lizzy hadn't had any success in getting to know Miss de Bourgh yet, but she did admire her clothes. Lizzy had not yet decided, however, if they displayed Anne's good taste or if the sartorial hand at work was Lady Catherine's. If so, Lady Catherine confined her good taste to her daughter's clothes. Her own were ostentatiously regal.

Anne shut her eyes almost before they were away from Rosings, with her mouth clenched into a fine line. Lady Catherine declared that they would be quiet for Anne's sake, so that she could sleep, and then proceeded to talk for a quarter of an hour.

The carriage was comfortable, though Lizzy would have preferred to have slightly more air. It was extremely well insulated. To think she should live to regret her family's drafty carriage!

Anne opened her shell-shaped vinaigrette, and the pungent smell of vinegar and perfume filled the air, filtering through the holes punched in the metal grill. It was rather overpowering in the close carriage; Lizzy could practically taste the vinegar in her mouth, reminding her of her mother's smelling salts.

The silence was also not improved by Lady Catherine's extended monologue on the state of the roads. But Lizzy wasn't one to repine, and eventually the de Bourgh ladies switched, with Lady Catherine dropping off to a doze and Anne sitting up.

Anne generally looked cross and uncomfortable, but today she looked genuinely pained.

"Are you... well?" Lizzy asked lamely.

Anne shifted, frowned, and snapped her vinaigrette shut. "I am never *well*."

"Is there anything I can do?"

"No. My head aches and the pain is traveling down my back and even to my..." She trailed off, looking embarrassed.

"Your legs?" Lizzy said.

Anne looked scandalized.

"Surely it's not improper to tell me that," Lizzy said with a smile. "There's no one to hear and I am your companion."

Anne sniffed. "I don't know what you imagine it means to be a companion, but vulgarity is not part of it."

Lizzy shrugged. "I am one of five sisters, you must remember. My youngest sister—"

Anne shook her head. "Please spare me the family anecdotes."

Lizzy sighed. No doubt Anne's pain was making her harsher than normal, but Lizzy doubted they would ever be friends. They had nothing in common, other than Charlotte.

"Would you prefer me to be silent?" Lizzy asked.

Anne pressed a hand to her forehead. "Yes. No. Oh, I don't know, but I wish I had a distraction."

"What pleases you to think about?" Lizzy asked, genuinely curious. "What is the happiest part of your life?"

For Lizzy, there were many to choose from. Her friendship with Jane, the special closeness with her father, her nieces and nephews...

Anne stared at the swaying ceiling as if Lizzy had asked her to complete a difficult sum. Eventually she lowered her eyes to Lizzy. "Are you trying to make my headache worse? Is it my fault my whole body aches? Why should I have to provide you with conversation?"

"I thought perhaps I could divert you, but I don't know what interests you."

Anne turned her face to the window and Lizzy temporarily gave up.

She did sympathize with the other girl's discomfort, but Anne wouldn't even try to think about something else. Lizzy couldn't understand that attitude. Did clinging to pain and discomfort make it easier to bear? Surely not. Maybe it was all Anne knew how to do.

Lizzy was relieved when the carriage reached Tunbridge Wells. It was a small spa town, and the carriage rattled cheerfully over cobblestones past stately brick buildings that housed the various hotels, health spas, and bath houses. A large plaza was dotted with ladies and gentlemen taking late-morning strolls. Many of them were elderly, though not all. They looked quite fashionable.

Their coach stopped at the very next hotel where a smart footman opened the door and handed the ladies out. The sun was hotter now than it had been. A welcome breeze fanned Lizzy's warm cheeks as she exited the carriage.

Mr. Darcy dismounted nearby and spoke with a groom before handing off the reins of his big, nut-brown mount.

Clearly, Lady Catherine's reputation preceded her, because the footman was already unloading the baggage tied on the back, and a stately woman came out to usher their party inside.

A private parlor was ready for them, and Lizzy, mindful of her duty, helped situate Anne near the fire. Why she would be chilled on such a warm spring day made no sense to Lizzy, but she had little experience of chronically sick persons.

Anne settled into the wing-back chair and rested her head back, closing her eyes. The room was brightly lit from two large windows which overlooked the street and a stately stone building on the far side. Claw-foot settees made a U in front of the fire, and behind them a glossy black table was set in preparation of tea.

Lady Catherine remained in the hall, speaking with the proprietress. Colonel Fitzwilliam and Mr. Darcy entered next, with a few spatters of mud on their boots. They went to the window and began to discuss the changes since they'd last been to the Wells.

Mrs. Jenkinson always put a cushion behind Anne's back, so Lizzy scanned the room and saw a similarly sized pillow on one of the settees. She brought it to Anne who automatically leaned forward so Lizzy could slide it behind her back.

Mr. Darcy watched her with a look of approval that Lizzy didn't appreciate. He had never approved of her before. Did seeing her in a lower position somehow right the balance of their social standing?

Or perhaps he was merely thinking how right he'd been to discourage Charles from pursuing Jane, now that Lizzy was a paid companion.

Oh, her father could not know what he had asked of her!

But Lizzy was made of stern stuff. If she could laugh away Darcy's stern *dis*approval, she could also laugh away his humiliating *a*pproval.

Anne sighed and pulled the cushion away without opening her eyes. "This one is like a rock."

Lizzy looked about. The other small cushions were the same. She grabbed her own shawl instead, rolled it into a neat bundle and touched Anne's shoulder again.

Anne sighed again when Lizzy slid it into place, but this time she leaned back comfortably.

When tea was brought, Lizzy poured, serving first Lady Catherine, then Anne, Colonel Fitzwilliam, and lastly himself, and Mr. Darcy couldn't take his eyes off her. Her movements were so sure, so composed. No needless fuss, like Caroline. No shy reserve, like his sister, Georgiana. Lizzy was everything that a young woman ought to be. Assured, but not arrogant, composed, but not insipid, lively, but not wild.

The liveliness only was lacking today. He wondered if the drive had disagreed with her. Stirred from his usual silence, he inquired while Lady Catherine turned her attention to Colonel Fitzwilliam.

"No, I'm never carriage-sick," Lizzy replied.

"Tired, perhaps?"

She looked bemused. "No, I am fine. Do I look ill?"

"It is only that you seem rather quiet."

"Quiet for *me*, you mean. I imagine that must be a relief for you."

Darcy frowned. "On the contrary."

Lizzy raised her eyebrows. "The silent Mr. Darcy asking for more chatter? Perhaps I have fallen asleep on the coach."

He colored slightly. This was not the time or place to discuss his feelings, but why did Lizzy think he wanted her to be quiet? "You do not merely *chatter*, as some women do. I am certainly not a great talker. That is… I do not find an easy flow with those who are not my particular friends.

But with you," he spoke more quietly, "my silence does not spring from disapprobation, but quite the opposite."

Lizzy blinked at him, then turned abruptly back to the tea settings. "Lady Catherine, do excuse me, I have forgotten to give the Colonel his cream."

Darcy frowned. Why her sudden discomfort? This was perhaps the first time he had spoken any of his approbation aloud, but she must have noted his preference for her company. Surely a simple comment would not cover her in confusion.

He did not have an answer before she accompanied Anne to her room.

{ 4 }

THE NEXT MORNING, BEFORE BREAKFAST, Anne felt faint and exhausted. She obediently followed her mother and Miss Bennet up the tree-lined Parade to the bath house where one had several options to consume the healing waters.

Anne shivered in the cold morning damp. Her mother was tireless. Elizabeth seemed always to be holding herself back from a run. But for Anne, it was currently a struggle to lift her toes high enough to avoid tripping on the flagstones. The sight of the broad steps up to the bath house made her wish to turn back or to sit upon them and cry, though she would never in a thousand lifetimes embarrass herself that way.

Anne had passed a poor night, not improved by the presence of her new companion. Yes, Elizabeth had gotten up several times when she heard Anne call, but she had not heard her every time.

Elizabeth had rotated the hot-brick in her bed with the one kept in the low-banked fire at least twice, but Anne had felt a creeping chill all night, along with cramps in her legs and aches in her back.

Elizabeth had held the teacup to her lips when Anne coughed dryly, but Anne could see the impertinent contempt in her eyes. She'd even offered to rub Anne's back with a laugh in her voice! She was so unfeeling. So happy in her serene world, untouched by pain or sorrow or difficulty!

Furthermore, Elizabeth seemed to think she was better than Anne. That grated. The second daughter of an undistinguished country gentleman, a girl who was now a paid companion... How could she possibly think herself above Anne, the daughter of Sir Richard de Bourgh? It was unimaginable, but there was something *off* about Elizabeth.

Anne missed Mrs. Jenkinson, who always knew what to do, and did not do it with a twinkle of laughter in her eyes. But thinking of Mrs. Jenkinson stung.

Anne had accidentally seen the first few paragraphs of a letter Mrs. Jenkinson wrote to her sister, the one she was to visit. It had... oh, it had not been complimentary to her! Mrs. Jenkinson "could not wait to get away from the oppression of Rosings," "unrelieved by Miss de Bourgh's sullen, ungrateful air." She was longing for "the cheerful company of real friends."

Anne had thought they *were* friends. She realized now that you could never truly be friends with someone you paid. Her mother had said that many times, but Anne had not realized how true it was.

Mrs. Collins, however... If she had come, how pleasant that would have been! She was such a calm, matter-of-fact woman. She allowed Anne to talk of her health and never seemed bored or contemptuous. She knew what it was like to have few options, and... and Anne liked her. Mrs. Collins was not paid, so any friendship between them must be real.

But no, instead of Mrs. Jenkinson or Mrs. Collins, Anne was settled with the boisterous, smirking Elizabeth Bennet.

Anne managed the steps and followed her mother into the columned building made of warm gray stone.

Elizabeth's worn shoes clicked on the polished tile as they entered, and the sound pierced Anne's head. Did Elizabeth even know how to walk quietly? Did she try?

"What large, modern windows," Elizabeth said. They were in a large central room with high ceilings. "They give such a light, airy feeling to the room. Why, I'm quite in love."

Anne found it too bright and too cold, but this was clearly the place to be before breakfast in Tunbridge Wells. It was nearly filled with the stylish visitors and residents of the Wells.

Many small, elegant groupings of chairs and settees were overflowing with well-dressed women and their companions. Morning tea was available for a small fee, but most were sipping the famous water from ornate, cut-crystal glasses. The water was drawn from the chalybeate spring, which was how Tunbridge Wells had earned its fame. Black-clad servers carried pitchers about and refilled the water as needed.

The doctor had informed Anne that she would need to start with two and half pints a day, building up to eight after two weeks. Anne could not imagine drinking half of such an amount.

She'd said as much, but to her intense surprise, her mother had scoffed at her. "Nonsense, Anne. Your health has robbed you of resolution, and I have been remiss in not pushing you further. You can and shall take the full course of waters."

Well. And then she'd saddled Anne with such a companion! Loud, laughing, grinning Elizabeth Bennet. Lady Catherine had even said that Elizabeth, for all her faults, had a great deal of resolution. Too much, Lady Catherine had added, but it was still the first time Anne's mother had compared Anne unfavorably to another woman. It had been a shock.

They were soon seated and Anne held her glass close to sniff it. There was a slight odor of rust.

"It is not at all distasteful," her mother assured her. "Not like the noxious brew they pass off as water in Bath. I myself have never tried it, but I am assured it is not to be compared." She looked up and upon catching the eye of an acquaintance, moved away to join them.

Anne sipped the water and grimaced. Not horrible, but rather cool and salty. Why could she not be required to drink two and half pints of hot tea? That would still be excessive, but not like this.

"Is it very awful?" Elizabeth asked.

"No," Anne said coldly. She drank again, managing two swallows. It was not so much salty as rusty. It made her mouth taste the way it did after one of her distressing nosebleeds.

"Well, you have my sympathy," Elizabeth said frankly.

Anne lifted her chin. "I'm not accustomed to receiving pity. Nor do I need it."

Elizabeth ought to respect her. Anne was the heiress of Rosings. What was she?

Elizabeth looked away, interesting herself in people-watching perhaps, as a small smile danced on her lips. Hopefully she would leave Anne in peace to finish her task.

Anne gulped some more water. When she was done they would return to the hotel for breakfast, and then stroll the Upper Parade with the gentlemen. Anne would prefer to lie down after breakfast, but her mother's new militant attitude would no doubt preclude that. It was recommended to walk after taking the waters, so walk they would.

Anne forced herself to down the last half of the glass. How demeaning to be forced to lap water like a horse. Her stomach revolted. Anne pressed a hand over her mouth. She must not humiliate herself by vomiting here!

Anne breathed slowly and deeply, trying to push her nausea down.

A server came and refilled her glass and the weight in her hand almost made her eyes fill with tears. She could not do this.

Without a word, Anne set the glass on a side table and stood blindly. She needed to go.

"Do you want me—" Elizabeth started.

"No," Anne snapped. Thankfully, her mother was already heading back toward her. In a low voice, Anne explained that she had drunk as much as she could.

"Nonsense," her mother said, in her normal loud voice. "I am sure I have every sympathy, but it is for your good, of course."

Anne responded, the tears gathering in her eyes. "Please, Mama, I am very unwell."

"No. Miss Bennet, please let me know when Anne's glass is empty. I wish to chat with Lady Mathilde before she goes."

Anne watched in consternation as her mother sailed off.

Her mother was never a source of sympathy, being herself so strong and healthy, but she had always had the utmost respect for Anne's delicacy. Until now.

Anne sat and picked up the glass. Years of obedience did not allow for anything else.

And yet... she felt so ill already!

Tears were on the point of falling.

Then Elizabeth astounded Anne by taking the glass in her own hand.

"May I?" she asked. Without waiting, she tipped up the glass and began to drink. When she sat it down, it was empty.

She made a slight face, but then inquired calmly, with a twinkle in her eye, "Shall I inform your mother the glass is empty? If she is still chatting, I'm sure I can escort you back to the hotel to lie down before breakfast."

Anne sat, in shock, as Lizzy did so, and soon they were heading slowly back down the street.

Anne could not bring herself to thank Lizzy for what she'd done. It was dishonest and brazen and impertinent.

But... it was also a relief. It was, Anne realized with a start, one of the kindest things somebody had done for her in a long time.

A quiet voice in Anne's mind urged her to say thank you, but it was not a voice she was accustomed to listening to.

"Why did you do that?" Anne asked finally. "You shouldn't have."

"Shouldn't I? I am terribly impulsive," Elizabeth admitted. "But I hate to see people suffer. Even—" She cut herself off.

"Even what?" Anne demanded. "Even people like me? Even people you despise?"

"No, not at all," Elizabeth said. "Even people who dislike me."

Anne was silent as they entered the hotel. She *did* dislike her new companion; she couldn't honestly say otherwise.

Elizabeth offered her arm to help Anne up the stairs to their adjoining rooms. "I don't despise you," she added kindly. "Why would I?"

Somehow Anne felt that Lizzy had missed the point. Now she spoke as if she pitied Anne! Anne was the *heiress of Rosings*.

Anne was relieved to reach her room, where she could take off her bonnet and pelisse and lie down to recover.

Only she wasn't sure what she was recovering from: the water or the conversation.

{ 5 }

LIZZY DID FEEL A LITTLE ODD after gulping a pint of water, but it was nothing a belated breakfast of toast, jelly, ham, and tea couldn't overcome. She was quite ready to walk afterward and was relieved to see Anne choke down two fingers of toast and gain some color in her face.

Lady Catherine had enjoyed a long tête-à-tête with her friend at the bath house and then discovered that Lady Mathilde was staying at the same hotel. Therefore, after breakfast Lady Catherine declared her intention of remaining behind and shooed the young people, including Colonel Fitzwilliam and Mr. Darcy, out to walk the Pantiles.

Colonel Fitzwilliam immediately offered his arm to Anne, so Lizzy was paired with Mr. Darcy. She had been unnerved by his sudden tone and style of talking the day before. She didn't know what to think, except that Charlotte's suspicions seemed a mite less ridiculous than before.

"I've heard of the Pantiles of Tunbridge," Lizzy said, wanting to set the conversation firmly on neutral ground, "but I wasn't sure this morning *which* tiles I should be admiring. I'm afraid all the paving stones look like plain rock to me."

"The pantiles were almost all replaced," Mr. Darcy explained, "about ten years ago. Perhaps fifteen. But there are still a few about. I'll try to find a few to point out to you."

He tucked her hand around his arm.

"Please do! I know the story about Queen Anne, of course, ordering it to be paved after her son tripped and fell, but I need to see the stones so that I can make the story at least partly about myself when I repeat it in Hertfordshire. That is the fun of sight-seeing, is it not?"

"The Wells are not so far from Hertfordshire. Have none of your acquaintance been here?"

"None that I can recall at the moment, though I daresay I'm wrong. Bath is much the more popular, so that is where we went when my mother wanted to take the waters."

"Did you enjoy Bath?"

Darcy was speaking so much more like a sensible man, easily holding up his end of the conversation, that she felt more in charity with him than she would have expected. "We went on the occasion of Lydia's first birthday, when I was…oh, five or six… so I don't have the clearest recollection. I mainly retain the image of rainy, cobblestone streets and a feeling of impatience."

"That sums up my feeling for Bath as well." He smiled at her so widely he almost—dare she say it—grinned. Lizzy was startled. It wasn't the sort of smile one gave to someone they looked down upon. It was a smile of… camaraderie?

"And where are we walking now?" Lizzy asked, looking away. "I mean, is it called the Parade or the Upper Walk? I have heard both."

"I believe it was renamed the Parade around the same time it was restricted to the gentry." The long walk sloped gently upward, lined on both sides by columned shops and homes. The buildings were neat and tidy, mostly a fresh white, with the occasional deep red or green painted trim. Sparkling windows fronted the walk, and Lizzy caught a quick reflection of herself and Mr. Darcy, looking rather modish, if she did say so herself. They'd passed Colonel Fitzwilliam and Anne, who naturally walked more slowly.

Lizzy and Mr. Darcy passed from the sun into the shade of a tall, elegant cypress, and Lizzy tipped her head back to look up at it. The trees were planted along the middle of the promenade, and the morning sun made an almost green glow beneath them.

"Whoever caused these trees to be planted just so ought to be rewarded." They left the shade and Lizzy laughed as the sun blinded her, quickly ducking her head. "I do not understand why Bath should be so in vogue, Tunbridge is adorable."

"Indeed, the High Weald is one of my favorite parts of England. You should… That is, if you ever get the chance, I believe you would enjoy visiting Ashdown Forest. Truly one of the wildest places left in the South, though it is only miles from here."

Lizzy laughed. "No. You will not make me believe that you prefer the dark, wild places to the neatness and utility of well-drained fields and good soil. I refuse to believe you to be a romantic."

"I did not say I was romantic. I have little patience for gothic novels and such works, but that does not mean that I may not appreciate nature when it is so blessed by the hand of Providence. Surely you agree?"

Their path brought them to a broad set of stairs that led to a higher walk. Lizzy and Mr. Darcy mounted them easily, looping around to the left to walk the upper length of the Parade. Lizzy was realizing that she was incapable of allowing a genuine attempt at conversation to go unrewarded, even if she did doubt Mr. Darcy's character. "If you are not trying to trap me into admitting my own preference for wildness, then I suppose I do agree. Have you ever been to the Lake District?" she asked in turn. "I hope to go this summer with my aunt and uncle, and I admit I was quite *aux anges* when they asked me."

"You will enjoy it tremendously, I expect. It is both stark and striking."

"Alliterative, Mr. Darcy. Almost poetic."

He was startled into a chuckle. "Accidental. I have no aspirations to poetry."

"No? That's probably wise. Nothing exposes a strong intellect to ridicule as effectively as poetry."

"As effectively as it starves love?"

Lizzy blinked. Did he remember that? She'd been embarrassed about her mother's hints to Bingley and Jane and jumped in with the first thing that came to mind. "As I recall, you countered that poetry was the food of love. Perhaps you are more poetic than you care to admit."

He looked away, his neck flushing slightly.

Lizzy looked and wondered and looked again.

"Perhaps we should wait here for Fitzwilliam and Anne," he said. They paused at a particularly good vantage point and he turned the conversation back to the Wells.

Lizzy listened with real interest to some of the tidbits of history she was not acquainted with. When the man deigned to speak, he was worth listening to. Mystified as she was, it was at least satisfying to understand how he had such good friends as Mr. Bingley. Truly, Wickham had been correct that he could be a pleasant and good companion when he so chose.

But thinking of Wickham and Bingley made her think of Jane, and she sighed inadvertently. "I wish Jane could be here. This truly is a charming town, if a trifle tame, and Jane would love every white-washed nook and cranny of it."

Lizzy expected Darcy to pass over the mention of Jane—there must be some trace of guilt, however proud he was!—but he nodded genially. "I'm sure Miss Bennet would enjoy Tunbridge. I'm thinking of fetching my own sister from London next week. I would be glad for you to become acquainted with her."

Lizzy opened her mouth twice before offering a lame, "Would you?"

Where had this smiling, courteous man come from? Was he experiencing sunstroke?

"Darcy!" A gentleman crossed from the other side of the walk, and Mr. Darcy and Lizzy turned to meet him. "I heard you were stopping here with your aunt." He slapped Darcy's shoulder.

Darcy, to her surprise, returned the gesture. "What are you doing here, Chuff? Shouldn't you be home in Buckinghamshire?"

"I was," he said cheerfully. "But Honoria hasn't been well since the babies. I convinced her to come down here but then she insisted she needed my escort. I was rolled up."

Darcy began to introduce Lizzy. "Allow me to present— "

"Your cousin!" His friend cut him off jovially. "No need to tell me. I'd heard you and she would make a match of it one day, and Honoria told me only this morning that

Lady Catherine and her daughter were fixed at the Holbourne Hotel with you. I was planning to visit."

Lizzy could feel her face flushing, and Darcy's arm under her hand stiffened to iron.

"Chuff!" called Colonel Fitzwilliam, coming up to them, with Anne on his arm. "How are you, old chap? Congratulations are in order, I hear. Twins, what?"

They congratulated him, but Darcy was still stiff when he did the introductions. "Allow me to present my cousin, Miss Anne de Bourgh, and her companion, Miss Elizabeth Bennet. Miss de Bourgh, Miss Bennet, this is my friend, Sir Charles Trevilian."

"A pleasure to meet you," Lizzy said, striving to quell a bubble of laughter. Could anything make Mr. Darcy more uncomfortable than the accusation of being engaged to her? Her slight apprehensions of the morning were relieved.

Sir Charles's eyes twinkled as he bowed over Anne's hand and then hers. "Pleasure is mine. I'll have to bring my wife over to make your acquaintance. She's a bit blue-deviled and a little lively distraction would do her good. Better yet, dinner!" He invited them all to sup at his hotel that very night before continuing on his way.

Mr. Darcy and Lizzy led on, again quickly outdistancing Anne and the Colonel.

Lizzy was not embarrassed—it was not *her* fault his friend had made such a contretemps!—but she was a little at a loss for further conversation.

"Sir Charles seems very jovial," she offered.

"Yes, he is a very good fellow. His wife, Honoria, is my second cousin."

"He reminds me somewhat of Mr. Bingley, or perhaps what Mr. Bingley may be like in ten years."

Darcy smiled again. Was that three times in one conversation? "I hadn't compared them, but I believe you may be right. Their temperament is similar. The same easy manners and sweet disposition. Chuff is not quite so impetuous as Bingley, but he is certainly not overly reflective. If Bingley marries well—"

Mr. Darcy broke off, for once looking shaken out of his proud stoicism.

Lizzy couldn't pretend she didn't know why he'd broken off. As they descended another set of stairs back to street level, he directed her attention to a fenced area off the lower walkway. "You were wondering about the Pantiles. Here is the original water well, the chalybeate spring, and the orange, square tiles around it are the original Pantiles. They were baked in a pan, hence the name."

Lizzy looked and admired, but she was indignant. How dare he talk to her about Bingley marrying well! She *knew* she and her sisters were somewhat ineligible, with their paltry thousand pounds each. Ugh, though they had not even that now, had they? Even if Darcy had not specifically detached Bingley from Jane, he was clearly glad the relationship had been scotched, and Lizzy was filled with renewed fury on Jane's behalf.

Bingley would never find a kinder, gentler, or more sensible woman than Jane! *Marry well,* indeed.

After Anne and the Colonel had admired the tiles and the spring, Lizzy managed to switch partners.

She was glad to walk on with Colonel Fitzwilliam while Mr. Darcy suited his steps to Anne's slower pace.

Clouds had come up, obscuring the sun and casting the whole length of the Parade into sudden gloom.

Colonel Fitzwilliam shaded his eyes as he looked at the clouds. "I shouldn't be surprised if we got a few drops." He looked back at Darcy and Anne. "I say, did Charles poke Darcy with his cane? He seems to have gone stiff as a rod."

Lizzy chuckled. "I believe Sir Charles mistook me for Miss de Bourgh. Just a misunderstanding."

The Colonel shot her a rather penetrating look. "Ah, no wonder."

"I suppose Miss de Bourgh does not have a wide acquaintance?"

"No, unfortunately she has been too ill for travel, and Rosings Park is very retired."

"And does she—I beg your pardon if I should not say so—but several times I have been told that she and Mr. Darcy are...that they are not exactly *affianced* but known to be intended for one another?"

He waved a hand as if warding off a fly. "No, no, he has no such intention. Miss de Bourgh will probably never be strong enough to be mistress of Pemberley. Or even to...well, don't let that worry you." He grinned. "You don't think he'd be making up to you if he was about to offer for his cousin, do you?"

Lizzy tripped and might perhaps have sprawled on the ground like Queen Anne's son if not for the Colonel's quick reaction to stabilize her.

"I beg your pardon," Lizzy said. "But that is not... you must be mistaken."

"Apology if I've over-stepped," he said. "I thought we'd become such good friends these past weeks at Rosings that I might venture... But I should beg your pardon. I speak too freely at times."

Lizzy was at pains to explain that she wasn't offended by his casual words, but rather that his conclusion was completely wrong. Either he did not believe her or refused to, and Lizzy was too mortified to make a bigger issue of it.

What a mess! Mr. Darcy had never expressed any admiration for her before yesterday—except perhaps a vague approval of her reading habits. But a man didn't propose to a woman because she liked to read! *What* was Colonel Fitzwilliam basing his idea on? And while she had shrugged off Charlotte's suggestion of Mr. Darcy's preference for her as the partiality of a friend, she couldn't make a similar claim on the Colonel.

Colonel Fitzwilliam was much more Mr. Darcy's friend than hers, so... so what did it mean? And how horribly awkward her position would be if he was correct! Mr. Darcy must needs ruin everything.

When she and Colonel Fitzwilliam reached the hotel, she immediately excused herself to her room.

{ 6 }

DARCY WAS STILL FEELING A LITTLE unsettled after they returned the ladies to the hotel. Chuff was a good friend but he'd stuck his foot in it today.

"Care for a ride?" Fitzwilliam asked. "Before my aunt returns for a luncheon?"

Darcy agreed. As they strolled to the stables at the south end of Tunbridge where they'd paid for their horses to be lodged, he replayed his conversation. He regretted that he'd said something about Bingley marrying as well as Chuff had done. He was certain Elizabeth didn't share her mother's mercenary aims toward Bingley, but that was badly said on his part. He merely meant that Chuff had married a sensible, elegant woman of superior understanding and that Darcy hoped as much for Bingley.

Jane did seem sensible enough, though a bit over fond of laughing. However, she didn't show any sign of being particularly attached to Bingley, or of being able to curb Bingley's carelessness or hasty decisions. Not to mention the vulgar behavior of her family, which would not do Bingley any favors as he strove to rise above his trade background.

They entered the stables and requested their horses be readied.

Fitzwilliam was looking at the fitful clouds, which were now making a patchwork of shade on the town. "Have you decided to stay a while? Or do we head back to London soon?"

"We shall stay. I'm going to fetch Georgiana here. Perhaps a change of scene will raise her spirits."

They mounted the horses and Fitzwilliam led the way south. "Would you like me to go for Georgiana? You don't have to forgo Miss Elizabeth's smiles for such an easy task."

Darcy was silent. Had he been that obvious? He was not a man to wear his heart on his sleeve. Having someone thus baldly state his secret state of mind was disconcerting and unpleasant.

"Oh come, Darcy," said Fitzwilliam. "I'm not making sport of you. Why should you not like her? And if you like her, why should you not court her? It's nothing to poker up about."

Darcy felt something in his chest relax ever so slightly. "You make it sound so... reasonable."

"I thought as much. You've convinced yourself there's a thousand and one obstacles, when it's really the simplest thing in the world. She's the daughter of a gentleman, yes? No great dowry, I expect, but that's nothing to you. She's obviously a lady, an intelligent young woman... Even Aunt de Bourgh likes her, against her will!"

Darcy laughed. "That is a triumph, indeed. Elizabeth is impossible to dislike." Darcy felt, as many quiet and reserved people tend to feel, a distinct lightening of spirits after having his reserve broken down. The steady light of Fitzwilliam's words was dispelling the dark shadows shrouding Darcy's secret wish. Suddenly it seemed quite possible and even respectable. Instead of feeling that he was indulging a selfish whim, he began to feel that he was making an unexceptionable choice.

Fitzwilliam continued, "I won't press you to say more. But I must add, Miss Bennet has no idea of your affection. I, who know you so well, can easily spot your attentions to her. She, on the other hand, does not."

Darcy frowned in thought. Surely she knew? He'd enjoyed the morning walk prodigiously. Elizabeth's alternate teasing and sincerity delighted him.

But she had seemed taken aback yesterday when he merely said he didn't disapprove her manner of talking. Darcy had just been shocked to realize that Colonel Fitzwilliam had guessed his intentions. Why on earth would he expect Miss Elizabeth to know?

In his secret soul, he realized, he already felt connected to Elizabeth. He expected her to read him better than his best friends and know him better than his family, but how foolish! However much he liked her, she did not, in fact, know him so well. She was a quick and observant girl, but not a mind-reader, and he would be an idiot to presume on the connection he felt to her.

It was not in his nature to confess an emotional realization to his friend, however, so he merely turned the conversation. But he tucked away the thoughts to ponder.

When next he saw Elizabeth, she was rested and dressed for dinner. Looking at her face closely, he realized now that she must have been tired this morning. The darkness under her eyes and tightness in her cheeks had gone away. Had she had a difficult night with Anne? He had not considered the more physical aspects of her companionship.

Trying to keep in mind his newly learned lesson, Darcy complimented her appearance with warmth.

Whatever he had expected, it was not for her eyes to narrow and the color to mount in her cheeks as if she were embarrassed or upset.

"Thank you," she said stiffly. "I must prefer Miss de Bourgh's gown tonight, however." She went into a glowing commendation of Anne's evening gown, which in turn made Anne look narrowly at her.

Lady Catherine smiled complacently. "Anne does have exquisite taste. It would not do for my generation, but I must say I think her taste excels the generality of young women of like age in all of England." Lady Catherine was overpowering in purple and feathers, which brushed the doorway when they left their hotel. She insisted Darcy escort herself and Anne, so Elizabeth fell back with the Colonel.

"Now, Miss Elizabeth would look very well in a bolder color," Lady Catherine commented. "Her features are too marked for that shade of pink that she wears tonight."

Darcy felt the impertinence of this remark, but Elizabeth only spoke up serenely from behind. "It originally belonged to my sister Jane. It suited her much better."

Lady Catherine snorted. "If you are reduced to wearing your sister's clothing, you need not boast of it."

"I only boast in having an unselfish sister with skillful fingers for alterations."

"Anne has the finest touch for embroidery," Lady Catherine said. "She has given it up these past years, but if the waters are helpful, she will soon have strength for those pursuits again."

Darcy felt a small quiver go through Anne at the mention of the waters, but all she said was, "Yes, Mama."

"Do you embroider, Miss Elizabeth?" Lady Catherine asked.

"No, ma'am. Not since I was very young, and those purses turned out ill."

"Ah, you should not have given it up. No proficiency is to be expected without great diligence. Young women want everything for nothing."

Darcy realized with a jolt that Lady Catherine was insisting on this prolonged comparison because of *him*. He might even be the whole motive behind this trip to Tunbridge that was supposed to strengthen Anne. He had never encouraged his aunt to believe that he would offer for Anne, but he had also never told her that he would not. It was beneath his interference.

At least it had been. Perhaps that needed to change.

In the private parlor of Chuff's suite, a larger table had been introduced to accommodate their party. Darcy didn't appreciate the cramped feeling he got from the overfilled space, but it was just like Chuff's easy nature to invite more people than he should merely because he enjoyed it.

His wife definitely felt the lack of space and apologized several times, but as she was indeed a woman of good sense, she soon put the best face on it. She ceased to apologize for something that was not her doing and focused on being an excellent hostess.

This she did by installing Lady Catherine at the head of the table and bestowing the other six in the happiest arrangement she could contrive. It left Darcy next to his aunt and two places from Elizabeth, which could not please him, but at least Elizabeth was on the opposite side of the table, nearest the foot, and he could watch her.

He did not mind the separation very much, for his mind was still full of the conversation from the morning. Someday, he imagined, he might have the privilege of sitting with her at Pemberley. Thinking such a thing, without the usual guilt and vacillation, was enough to buoy his mood for the entire evening. He endured his aunt, laughed with his friend, and kept up with a witty update from his cousin, Lady Honoria.

"Darcy," she said at the end of the final course, "you are most lively tonight. I don't believe I've seen you like this since your father... well, for many years."

She apologized with her eyes for referring to his parent's death in that way, and he smiled to set her at ease.

When his eyes flicked to Elizabeth, he was surprised to find her, for once, looking at him. She looked perplexed, with a troubled, confused stamp about her eyes and forehead. Darcy instinctively smiled at her as well, and she looked away.

{ 7 }

LIZZY ENJOYED THE DINNER PARTY despite herself. If she'd formed any expectations at all, it was that she would feel low and humbled during her first dinner with strangers who knew her only as "Miss de Bourgh's companion," but that was far from the case. Colonel Fitzwilliam was always a gentleman, and her other partner, Sir Charles, was most affable.

Also, she was seated far from Lady Catherine.

When Lizzy made a chance comment about Mr. Bingley, answering a question from Colonel Fitzwilliam, Sir Charles immediately demanded to know how they were acquainted. From there he made quick work of learning the story of the summer, and that Lizzy had met Mr. Darcy long before she'd met Lady Catherine. Lizzy couldn't help looking at Mr. Darcy as she explained. Today he had been friendly and talkative beyond what she had ever seen. He was like a different man, and it confused her.

Then he turned to look at her and smiled. She stumbled to a stop.

Sir Charles had a decided twinkle in his eye when he asked if she had yet visited Pemberley, which Lizzy laughingly negated, determined to change the subject. "I am sure it is beautiful, but I am still entranced with Tunbridge. I have scarce learnt it yet."

"If you walked the Pantiles, you've seen most of it," he said.

"But I've only walked it once, in mid-morning," Lizzy protested. "I must see it by sunrise, for I believe the east light would change the trees entirely. And mid-afternoon with a wind, when the shadows are dancing, would also be necessary. Then sunset, of course."

He laughed with delight. "Don't forget starlight. When the lamps are extinguished."

"Of course! And then I should like to see the leaves spinning down like a shower in a strong wind. And if I had an umbrella, I do believe I should need to take the Upper Walk during a rain. Then perhaps, I might feel my trip to Tunbridge complete."

He laughed again. "You have high goals, ma'am."

Anne, who had been sitting silently to his right, suddenly cut in. "I don't know why you should wish to be always out of doors. If you have seen it once, you can surely imagine those scenarios."

Sir Charles turned to her with a smile. "No doubt she could. And how are you liking the Wells, Miss de Bourgh? Have you tried the waters yet?"

She shot a glance at Lizzy, who was rather shocked to see a look of resentment on Anne's face. Why should Anne resent her?

"Yes, the water is tolerable, I suppose. How does your wife like it?"

"Oh, she says they make her feel vile in the morning, but once she switched to the afternoon it was much better. In fact, she said— "

But he was interrupted by the sound of a baby crying in a nearby room.

The muffled sounds of a nursemaid were also heard, and then another set of small lungs let off a wail.

Lizzy watched with interest as Lady Honoria clapped her hands. "The twins are awake. In London, I would not bring them out, but among such close friends, I cannot resist. Do retire to the fire, and I will bring them in. Just for a moment."

The small party rearranged themselves to the settees by the fire, while the waiters came to empty the table. Lady Catherine naturally took the largest, throne-like chair, and Anne was nearest the fire, but how Lizzy came to be sitting next to Mr. Darcy she was not at all sure.

"Do you like infants, Miss Elizabeth?"

"Not as much as I like ewes and kittens," she admitted. "But then, my aunt's children were delightful babies, so I suppose it depends. I hope to be a good aunt to my sisters' children someday."

Lizzy truly hadn't meant to bring up Jane again, but she couldn't help it! Her sisters were an integral part of her life and she couldn't edit them out.

"Georgiana is the only infant I had experience with. And she was appealing, though quite bald until she was two. I was concerned."

Lizzy laughed in spite of herself. "How old were you?"

"I am twelve years her senior. It seemed to me quite a tragic problem for a girl, but no one seemed to notice. I was much relieved when her hair came in."

Lizzy laughed again and Mr. Darcy's eyes warmed at having made her do so.

Then the babies with their long white gowns were brought in by Lady Honoria and two nursemaids.

Lady Catherine held up a hand. "Not too near me, if you please. Infants are always damp and often dirty, and I must deprecate the decision to bring them out. If I had been consulted, I would have strongly urged otherwise."

Even Anne shrank slightly at this rude speech and Lady Honoria's full lips wobbled. Lizzy stood abruptly. "What beautiful boys! May I hold one?"

Honoria came to Lizzy and Darcy vacated so she might have his spot. Soon Lizzy was holding Andrew, "after my

grandfather," Lady Honoria explained, and Colonel Fitzwilliam was holding Tracy, "after Chuff's grandfather."
The baby was light and warm and his bright blue eyes were
fixed on her face quite intently.

Lizzy unexpectedly felt tears gathering in her eyes. She
was not a nostalgic or overly sentimental girl, but when she
thought of how much Jane wanted this, it hurt. Lizzy could
barely imagine snuggling her own baby someday, but Jane
had begun to indulge concrete daydreams of motherhood,
and to think of Jane's current disappointment was painful.

Lizzy quickly mastered the impulse without a single
tear escaping and complimented Honoria on all the excellent qualities of her baby, including his height, weight, volume, and obvious intelligence.

The baby squirmed such that his cap fell off, and
Honoria stooped to retrieve it. Andrew's small downy head
was quite bald, and Lizzy accidentally made eye contact
with Darcy, whose lips twitched suspiciously like a
chuckle.

Soon it was time for the babies to retire. Lady Catherine
breathed a sigh of relief.

"But I cannot be easy until you both wash thoroughly,"
she told Lizzy and the Colonel. "I am sure I heard one of
them cough and I do hope Anne has not been infected."

Lizzy's lip curled. Lady Catherine was solicitous of
Anne's health, but she must have been the coldest mother

to infant Anne! Perhaps it was not shocking that Anne seemed stiff and unfriendly.

When they took their leave, Lizzy found herself on Darcy's arm this time. Chuff had volunteered to walk them back, and he escorted Lady Catherine ahead of them, while Colonel Fitzwilliam supported Anne.

The night was dark and chilly now, with a damp that seeped into her shoes.

"There are not many stars, I'm afraid," Darcy said.

Lizzy glanced up. It was indeed cloudy, though a ghostly moon illuminated one patch of coiling mist and provided some light beyond the low yellow streetlamps.

He continued, "Perhaps I might also walk with you tomorrow afternoon or evening, to help you complete your experience of Tunbridge."

Lizzy was not surprised that he'd heard part of her conversation, but his whole tone—affectionate? deferential? —filled her with unease. Was he asking to *walk out* with her in a romantic way? Under his aunt's nose? Surely not!

In a cool tone, she replied, "I believe Miss de Bourgh will be resting then, and may require my help."

"Ah, of course. But perhaps sometime when she is otherwise occupied? I would like—and I apologize for the unorthodox timing of this announcement—to court you."

Lizzy's eyes flew toward Lady Catherine, but that lady was some distance ahead of them. Darcy had been purposefully falling behind, she realized, so that they would not be overheard.

His statement was not quite the shock it would have been a week before, but it was still enough to render her acutely uncomfortable.

He continued. "I have admired you since our acquaintance began in Hertfordshire, and on becoming better acquainted with you during your stay at Hunsford, I decided I need not allow the scruples that have held me back to prevent me from speaking. I was even glad that my aunt requested you to accompany Anne, as it gave me more time with you. You..." he cleared his throat. "You are the reason that I came here at all."

She kept her face forward. "I don't think... That is..."

"Have I surprised you so much? I was afraid I might. Colonel Fitzwilliam warned me as much. As you can imagine, raising your hopes before I had any true intention of pursuing you was the last thing I desired. As I am now certain, I wanted to take the first opportunity to make you aware of my intentions."

"Raising my *hopes*..." Lizzy choked a little. He could hardly have displayed more complacent pride in look and tone if he had tried. "I'm afraid I must tell you at once that I do not believe we should... suit. I have no current thoughts of matrimony."

Now it was Darcy's turn to be taken aback. "But surely... now that I have told you, the matter is different.

You mustn't think this is a thoughtless impulse on my part. I would never insult you or myself by such impetuosity. I have given this great thought, and though my scruples on the character of your family and position of your relatives have long prevented me from speaking, I have decided that it is not an insurmountable barrier to a courtship."

Lizzy felt her face growing hot. A few weeks ago, she would have given him a scathing set down and felt none the worse for it. But somehow he had slipped under her guard the last few days, with his unexpected dashes of humor and even briefer flashes of self-awareness. Lizzy loved to laugh, and she realized with dismay that there was no better way to her heart than to make her smile.

In short, she had begun to soften her attitude toward Mr. Darcy, and his harsh words about her situation stung all the more.

"Thank you for the explanation, but it is unnecessary," she said. "I must repeat that I do not think we should suit. I'm sure the scruples which held you back will soon make you think better of it. I am your cousin's *paid companion* after all. This is completely improper."

Her hand rested still on Darcy's arm and she felt him tense.

"But surely that is all the more reason that you would want to accept—" He cut himself off, but it was painfully obvious what he had been thinking.

Lizzy now felt mortified. "I know it is a truth universally acknowledged that a woman must be delighted to accept a man so much her superior in rank and wealth, but surely you are not suggesting that I accept you for monetary reasons? You insult us both."

"Not at all," Darcy said stiffly. "I would never want a wife under such terms."

"Nor I, a husband."

"That is it? I do not even merit your regret at refusing me?"

"You have not made an offer, so I am not exactly refusing you. I am merely informing you, in the absence of my father or mother, that a courtship is out of the question."

"And why is that? Truly?" There was offended pride in the question, but also an undercurrent of real disappointment. She was well-enough acquainted with him by now to hear it.

As such, her next answer was softer than it might have been, though still uncompromising. "If you must know, I could never consider a relationship with someone who doesn't value my family and has intentionally done them harm. Jane is, even now, nursing a broken heart. That injury was at least partly your doing. And when I consider your behavior to Wickham, I cannot conceive how I could ever respect you enough to marry."

At this, his free hand closed over hers, gripping tightly. "You seem very interested in that man's welfare. He ought to be completely beneath your notice."

"Why? Because he is poor? Because you do not like him? Must I remind you that I also may be poor one day?" Perhaps she already was, if her father's investments were as bad as he thought.

Darcy released her hand and dropped her arm. "You need not. And this is what you think of me? Good heavens. I am surprised you would walk so far with my escort. My apologies, Miss Bennet."

They were only a stone's throw from the arched entry to their hotel, and they walked back together, yet separately.

Anne complained of pain with her breathing, and Lizzy quickly led her away, with her own cheeks still burning.

{ 8 }

DARCY LEFT THE HOTEL AS SOON as Lady Catherine was taken back to their parlor. He shook off Chuff and the Colonel and strode out alone.

What had just happened? It was like a nightmare to be plunged from his dream of happiness straight into that frightful conversation with Elizabeth. Her tone—so chilled! Her eyes—so angry!

One moment she was holding a baby, smiling at him in a way that made him want to kiss her in front of the whole party. The next moment she was telling him that she had no respect for him.

Darcy was a man who rigorously controlled his moods, even as a child, and it was a rare disappointment that caught him in the gut like this.

He had not nearly discharged his spleen by the time he reached the end of the Upper Walk. He was too sensible to think of staying out all night, or anything of that nature.

The smallness of Tunbridge Wells did not lend itself to the kind of long, punishing walk he could have indulged in London. All too soon he had looped back around to their hotel.

Unfortunately for his stronger emotions, his innate sense of justice was reasserting itself. Elizabeth was wrong about Wickham, but she did not know the truth. He hadn't even made her choose between Wickham's account and his own. He had given her nothing.

Honestly, he ought to be thankful Wickham had not imposed more wickedly on the Bennet family and the Hertfordshire community than indulging in a fit of slander. If Wickham had injured Elizabeth or her sisters, Darcy would be entirely to blame! The militia would soon move on from Hertfordshire to Brighton—after being so unpleasantly startled by Wickham's appearance, Darcy made certain to keep himself apprised of the man's whereabouts—otherwise, he probably ought to consider exposing the man publicly.

As for Jane, he did not know the elder Miss Bennet well, and while he would like to think Elizabeth was being overly dramatic in describing her as broken-hearted, he could not assume she was wrong.

He also thought of the Colonel's words from earlier. Something about only seeing Darcy's affection because he knew him. It was only logical to assume Elizabeth understood her sister, and that Darcy had been wrong when he arrogantly depended on his own slight observation to gauge the lady's affection.

Darcy sighed. Before he went up to his room, he went to the taproom and requested paper and ink. He had a letter to write.

He'd written only a page however, when a servant boy came running past their private parlor.

"Here, what's going on?" Darcy demanded, now realizing that there had been a number of fast footsteps going past the door for some minutes. "A doctor for the lady, the sick lady!" he told Darcy breathlessly. "They wants him."

Darcy flipped the paper over. "For Miss de Bourgh? You look dead on your feet already. I'll accompany you."

The boy nodded. "Yes, sir. If you want, but we must go."

Lizzy had found that Anne was indeed unwell. She wheezed distressingly and at times her lips seemed to turn nearly blue. Lizzy had finally knocked on Lady Catherine's door, rapidly and loudly.

"I think we must call a doctor for Anne," she called.

Lady Catherine's abigail opened the door with a frown. "Her ladyship has gone to bed."

"I can't stay," Lizzy said. "But ring immediately for a man to go for the doctor."

She rushed back to Anne's room. Anne was leaning heavily on the arm of a chair, facing the fire. She seemed to be trying to remain calm, but her thin chest shuddered with each breath.

She'd told Lizzy another day that heat helped her lungs, so Lizzy added another log to the fire. She burnt her hand slightly when she grabbed the tongs. She had stupidly left them in the fire earlier. Sucking a finger, Lizzy hovered uncertainly near Anne.

She was no doctor and feared to do the wrong thing. Her instincts urged her to touch Anne, to hold her hands or somehow lend her comfort, but her actual relationship with Anne was so poor, she doubted Anne would be comforted by her.

Lizzy wished for Jane. No, better yet, her Aunt Gardiner. She was such a calm, motherly woman.

When Anne's arm slid off the edge of the chair and she slumped forward, Lizzy couldn't take it any longer.

She knelt before Anne and grasped both her forearms. She gently guided her back to an upright position, and then began to chafe her hands, talking soothingly.

"Just relax. The doctor will be here soon. Not to worry. Your mother is getting help and soon you will be peacefully in bed. Just breathe, nice and easy."

Lady Catherine's maid came and went, but Lizzy stayed focused on Anne, whose breathing gradually eased. Only later did she realize that not once did Lady Catherine come to see how her daughter fared in person.

When Darcy opened the door and let the doctor enter, Lizzy was relieved, though she felt Anne was out of immediate danger.

Once the doctor had arrived, Lady Catherine came as well. She greeted the man by name, introducing herself "from our correspondence." The man seemed to know already about Anne and had brought several cloth bags of powders.

"I've been reading about the effects of an infusion of iron in a similar case of severe chronic cough and debilitation." He mixed three dark grains into a small vial.

Lady Catherine described Anne's attack as though she had been there, so Lizzy could only assume this was commonplace. What a sad state of affairs for Anne! Now that her mother, the doctor, and two maids were in the room, Lizzy slipped away. She needed to regain her composure after the tense anxiety of the past half hour. Also, due to rushing about and kneeling next to the roaring fire, she was unpleasantly damp with her own perspiration.

In the parlor hired by Lady Catherine, there was still the remains of tea service, which must have been overlooked in the commotion. She served herself a lukewarm cup and sat shakily for a moment. A paper lay upside down on the small adjacent desk and she idly turned it over.

To her surprise, it was addressed to her. Though unfinished and not yet signed, it clearly was from Mr. Darcy's pen.

With dismay, she found herself perusing the sheet, reading his account of his dealings with Bingley, and the beginning of an explanation about Wickham, something involving his sister.

With a guilty start, she replaced the paper exactly where it had been.

Mr. Darcy would no doubt return to finish this letter at any moment, and she did not wish to see him.

Leaving her half-drunk cup of tea, she fled back towards her tiny bedroom.

When Darcy returned some ten minutes later and sat to finish writing, he would swear that he could smell Elizabeth. It was most unsettling, and he could only ascribe it to his complete failure to control his infatuation, despite the severe check it had received tonight. With a sigh, and a last involuntary sniff, he resumed his writing.

{ 9 }

IN THE MORNING, LIZZY FOUND that Mr. Darcy was gone. He had returned to London as planned to fetch his sister.

A servant brought the letter to her after breakfast. Anne was keeping to her room after the previous night's attack, and so Lizzy was restricted to the hotel. In the country, she would walk out for peace and solitude while reading it, but Lady Catherine had informed her it was improper to walk out alone in Tunbridge. Lizzy was less than convinced, but as a companion, she'd resigned herself to staying within most of her employer's guidelines. She was comforted to know that if her situation became unbearable, it would be downright easy to get Lady Catherine to turn her off. Lizzy need merely walk out alone, speak too freely in company, or say any one of the things she *actually* thought about Lady Catherine to her face.

Resigned to staying in, Lizzy pulled the blinds back to let in the morning sunlight from the hotel side yard and forced one of the windows open to allow a slight breeze to sneak into the warm room.

Her fingers trembled slightly with the catch. Her emotions were decidedly not tranquil. She needed Jane to talk her into equanimity.

Pulling the letter out and smoothing the pages on the escritoire, she began it warily. It looked like he had rewritten it from the previous version. He had transposed the order of his explanation and taken out some of the more emotional statements he had made. It felt strangely intimate to see the second draft, to see what he had sought to conceal or mitigate.

Dear Miss Bennet,

Do not fear that I mean to recite those same sentiments which so disgusted you this evening. I will not importune you or further lacerate either of our hearts.

However, you pointed out several objections to my character, which I feel I must explain, both for my peace of mind and your future safety.

The first misunderstanding, and in my mind by far the most severe, is the nature of my dealings with George Wickham.

Lizzy bit her lip savagely. What could he dare say about his treatment of that gentleman? But as she read on, concerning Wickham's greed, ungratefulness, debauchery, and eventual attempt to ensnare Miss Darcy into an elopement, Lizzy's certainty faded to a whisper. She did not want to believe it. She scoffed at Mr. Darcy's apology for not doing more to protect the ladies of Meryton from Wickham.

But then she thought of Miss King, the heiress Wickham had dangled after, and grimaced uncertainly.

When she read again of Mr. Darcy's dealings with Bingley and Jane, and her own family's mortifying behavior at the Netherfield Ball, she darted to her feet with too many suppressed emotions to contain. She paced her room, alternately burning with embarrassment and cold with anger. She felt all the worse for being stifled in her room. Oh, what she would give for a long walk in the country!

Unable to burn off her nervous energy, she read again, and again.

With every reading, his words became more plausible. With every reading, her own conduct grew more questionable. What exactly had Mr. Wickham ever done to secure her approbation? He had complimented her, preferred her to others, that is until Miss King received her inheritance, but that was nothing. She wracked her mind for an instance of his disinterested kindness, honesty, or diligence… and could think of nothing. In fact, she now saw much in his behavior to deplore. Surely it was indiscreet to pour his whole history into her ears on such slight acquaintance? And though he had said he held the elder Mr. Darcy in great respect, he had certainly slandered the son with impunity when there was no danger.

One recollection led to another, and Lizzy was brought low. She had to admit that neither Darcy nor Wickham now appeared to be what she'd thought them. Even worse, she had to admit how much her vanity had exposed her to ridicule. She was no better than her mother, or Lydia!

She reread the end of Darcy's letter and took little comfort from it. Yes, she and Jane had been "above reproach," but that did not lessen the sting of the criticism of her family.

Even the last paragraph failed to comfort her.

I apologize again for anything that could hurt you in this explanation. It is not, nor has it ever been, my intention to mortify or wound you, and it pains me to do so now. I realize that I have been much at fault, and I hope that you will forgive me.

Yours sincerely,
Fitzwilliam Darcy

A sharp knock at the door roused her. Lizzy was almost relieved to be called to attend Anne. Anything was better than more solitary reflection.

In waiting on Anne, and being forced out of herself, Lizzy was insensibly cheered. Hers was a naturally optimistic spirit, and she began to wonder if possibly her outburst to Mr. Darcy would have a good result for Jane.

Perhaps Mr. Darcy would admit to Mr. Bingley that he had been mistaken!

But Lizzy's feelings were volatile and rose and sunk repeatedly. By the time she could retire to bed, and she sat at her desk to write to Jane, the blank paper mocked her. She desperately needed a confidante, but Jane was too close to the heart of the matter.

Lizzy sighed, pushed away the ink stand, and crawled into her bed. She hoped Anne had a good night's sleep, because Lizzy was sure she herself would sleep through any disturbance.

Thankfully, that was the case, and Lizzy felt much restored the next day. Lady Catherine said that Anne was also much better—though Anne's severe pallor didn't do much to back up this statement—and that they should all go to the pump room again so that Anne might continue to drink the waters.

Lizzy saw Anne dart a glance at her. Did she still resent Lizzy's interference with the water? Or was she hoping Lizzy would help her again? Lizzy certainly wouldn't, unless Anne specifically requested her help.

Who *would* Anne turn to if she were distressed? She had suffered a severe attack only two days ago, and yet, whom did she talk to? Had she ever confided in anyone? Her life was so lonely. Lizzy had thought the young lady was intended for Darcy, but clearly he did not think so. Would Anne be alone her whole life?

Lizzy was still pondering Anne's lonely predicament when they settled themselves onto one of the shiny settees in the posh pump room. Anne sat stiffly, face pinched and petulant, not looking at all lonely. She was so hard to like! And why should Lizzy try so hard to like her?

With a guilty start, Lizzy realized she was trying harder because of Mr. Darcy. She had judged him unfairly and never reconsidered, and so she was trying to reconsider Anne. Lizzy smiled ruefully at herself. Maybe she could learn to withhold judgment, and maybe not, but at least she laughed at her own foibles and weaknesses as well as those of others.

"What are you laughing about?" Anne snapped. She had just received her first glass of water.

"Myself," Lizzy answered candidly. "I am… a most inconsistent person, I find. And sometimes there is nothing to be done but laugh."

Anne's sour expression grew more pinched. "I can't drink this with you smirking so."

Lizzy spread her hands. "Is there any way you might view me as a friend, Miss de Bourgh? I do not know what I have done to offend you."

"Friends? You act as though you are… above me."

"Do I? I do *not* think that, though I suppose I do think my life has been more fortunate than yours." Lizzy saw her brow descend and hastened to add, "It is not pity, only… sympathy."

"You? Mrs. Collins sympathizes. You laugh."

"I do love to laugh, but never at *you*! I know I have not been so ill-bred. Mrs. Collins and I have been close friends all our lives. Perhaps for her sake you could give me a chance."

"But Mrs. Collins knows what it is to... be unwanted, to suffer," Anne blurted out. "What do you know about it? You are pretty and lively and... oh, please go away."

Lizzy could not think what to say. She stood and drifted toward the windows overlooking the street. Was it true that she did not know suffering? She had annoyances to bear in her mother and sisters, but that was not *suffering*. She had hurt along with Jane at Bingley's abandonment, but that was Jane's tragedy, not Lizzy's.

She had never contemplated Charlotte's lot as *suffering*, but... would Charlotte have considered Mr. Collins without severe provocation? Charlotte's family loved her, but they were not wealthy, and her status there as she grew older would only have decreased.

Lizzy leaned her forehead against one of the huge windows that let in large bars of watery sunlight. She craved the sun and the outdoors here.

Lizzy liked to think that she held to her standards of marriage, including true love and esteem, out of idealism and strength of will. But was it just that she had never suffered enough to compromise?

Nearby, on a bench lit by another window, there was a fond mama and a little boy in an old-fashioned costume who looked disgruntled. A portraitist was capturing their likeness, with an easel and at his feet an open box of oil paints, brushes, and powders.

Lizzy watched him work for a few minutes, as several others were doing. Lady Catherine could not leave her in peace, however. She soon made her imperious way to Lizzy and gestured with a jerk of her head to Anne. "I don't pay you to ignore my daughter, Miss Bennet."

"Anne asked for a moment of privacy to drink the waters. I am obliging her as best I can." Lizzy couldn't help the bite in her voice or her raised eyebrows.

Lady Catherine tapped her cane on the marble floor. "You're much too confident in yourself, as I've told you. Young women must learn to respect their elders. Come."

Lizzy's lips tightened as she followed Lady Catherine back toward Anne. How vulgar it felt to be treated this way!

Lizzy was sorting through retorts, but Lady Catherine didn't wait. "My nephew is coming back tomorrow."

This seemed a non-sequitur. "Indeed."

"Don't *indeed* me. I know why you accepted this position. You were inching your way into his affection during your entire visit with the Collinses. I daresay you would have accepted my offer even if I hadn't offered a salary."

Lizzy gaped. She felt really ill with disgust. "How dare you—"

"I *dare* because that is exactly why I asked you to join us. I know you flirt with him, and he prefers you, but I won't have you think me a fool or a dotard. You are exactly the sort of lively, spirited girl who gentlemen like Darcy and the Colonel admire. *Admire,* mind you, I don't say marry. But I saw at once that Darcy would come if you did, and I'm nothing if not a strategist. I daresay if I had had the handling of Bonaparte, I could have saved a good many lives."

Lizzy was struck temporarily dumb.

"Where was I?" Lady Catherine said. "Yes. I am willing to sponsor you on this little jaunt, but only because I have the utmost confidence in my nephew's character. Darcy may admire you, and he may linger here to enjoy your company, but he will do what honor requires. I drop a word of warning in your ear, for though I deplore your independent demeanor, I do not dislike you, precisely. Indeed, I have told Anne that she would do well to observe your manner."

"Then I am – I am bait?" Lizzy stuttered with anger and mortification. "I wonder that you should admit to such a motive. It's shameful. And I can only add that I have absolutely no designs on your nephew."

Lady Catherine gave a smug smile. "If so, well for you. Darcy will never ask you."

Lizzy was burningly angry now. "Indeed, he asked me to consider courtship only two days past. I *refused* him."

Lady Catherine's face changed color and Lizzy's did as well. She should not have said that; she should not have revealed it. But Lizzy was impetuous, and anger was her downfall.

"I only hope you will pay me the respect to never mention this again. Excuse me." Lizzy swept blindly away.

It had felt low to accept a paid, menial position, but that was *nothing* to this. Mortification was too mild a word.

Lizzy's immediate thought was departure. She could not stay where she would be so demeaned, where Lady Catherine would treat her as... almost as a trollop! She would leave. She would use her meager funds to take the Mail to London to her aunt and uncle and Jane.

Oh, to see Jane! Heaven!

But... reality came back to her in the form of a matron's lingering side glance. Lizzy could not pace angrily in a public place. She controlled herself with a supreme effort and pretended that she needed to speak with the *maître d'hotel.* (She asked for another cup of water for Miss de Bourgh, with a bit of vindictive satisfaction.)

She returned slowly to Anne's part of the room. Lizzy could not simply disappear from her post. It would cause talk, and worse, it would be weak to flee Lady Catherine in such a way. It would be weak to avoid speaking to Darcy after the revelation of his letter.

She was not respected here, true, but was she so very respected at home? Not by her mother or her younger sisters, that was sure. Her father, yes, but then, hadn't he been the one who asked her to accept this position? Yes, he was depressed by his loss of finances, but her stay with the de Bourghs didn't materially change that situation.

Lizzy sat down by Anne, and this time, did not wonder at Anne's sour expression. If Lady Catherine had held Lizzy up as a model to emulate, of course Anne would resent her.

Lizzy did *not* offer to drink Anne's water.

Darcy escorted Georgiana and her companion into the hotel with his usual calm manner, though it was only skin deep.

He was not worried that he would betray himself by any unseemly display of emotion now or in the coming days, but outward stoicism was not enough for him. He would not be satisfied with himself until he was *internally* indifferent to Elizabeth's presence.

He hoped, obviously, that his letter would clear up some of Wickham's slander, but he did not expect any more. She had made her position clear, and he was familiar enough with women (through his sister and aunts) to know that winning an argument was in no way related to winning a woman's affection or good will. In fact, quite the opposite.

He had very much considered writing to Lady Catherine that he and Georgiana were needed at Pemberley instead of returning to Tunbridge Wells, but he felt such a move was beneath him. It would be weak to change his plan merely because of a matter of the heart. It would be weak to avoid Elizabeth when she might reasonably guess why he had disappeared.

No, he would follow his plan of bringing Georgiana to Tunbridge Wells. He would regain his serenity, and after a suitable, hopefully short, interval, they would leave.

A secret voice whispered that he would not regain serenity so much as loneliness when he left, but he did not choose to listen.

In the private parlor, Elizabeth was plumping a pillow behind Anne's back. A book was set open on her chair, and a warm fire glowed in the hearth. It was a pleasing picture of domesticity, and when Elizabeth turned towards them and smiled, though it was obviously strained, Darcy had to clear his throat.

Good Lord. What had he done, coming back here?

Lady Catherine came in from her room, having been informed of their arrival, and Anne rose to greet Georgiana. In the commotion of greeting and removing coats and pelisses, Elizabeth disappeared out the door to the stairs.

Darcy found himself feeling empty without her presence, even as the Colonel joined them and teased Georgiana about the sketchbook always clutched in her hand.

There was liveliness and ease and... he should be *glad* that Elizabeth wasn't always present with the family. It would be far less awkward this way.

He was not glad.

Lizzy could not yet face Mr. Darcy. There warred within her too much new information and too much uncertainty. There was his letter—oh, that maddening and unexpected letter—besides Lady Catherine's shameless warning. Then there was Lizzy's own mad imprudence in blurting out the truth to Lady Catherine.

If Lady Catherine spoke of it to Mr. Darcy—oh! It would be beyond mortifying. Would he think she'd been boasting about his offer? Or taunting his aunt?

Lizzy, who had deplored Lydia's complete lack of discretion, was red with the knowledge of how thoroughly hers had failed in this instance.

Her tiny room was more claustrophobic than ever, knowing that Mr. Darcy was just downstairs, along with his tall, handsome sister. What wouldn't she give to take back those five minutes with Lady Catherine!

And beyond that, how ought she to act with Mr. Darcy? She felt an apology was owed him, both because of her blurting out his business to his overbearing aunt, and because of her original, harsh rejection. Although she still did not feel any affection for him, she had to admit that her judgment of his character had been unmerited and prejudiced. While he was in Tunbridge, she should offer an apology. After that... hopefully he and his sister would not stay long.

A knock on her door interrupted her reverie, and when she answered it, Lizzy was relieved to see it was only Miss Darcy's middle-aged companion. She looked a warm, matronly woman, not nearly so stiff and proper as Lizzy would have expected.

"How do you do?" the lady said politely. "I wanted to introduce myself to you. I am Mrs. Annesley, and you are Miss Bennet?"

"That's right. Please call me Lizzy or Elizabeth though, if you please."

"You have the look of a Lizzy," she smiled. "I will be in the adjacent room to you here, across from Miss Darcy. Please let me know if I can serve you in any way. I understand you have never been a companion before, and I would be pleased to offer any help I may, without overstepping."

Coming from anyone else, Lizzy might have felt defensive after this little speech, but Mrs. Annesley was so deferential, with such an understanding light in her eyes, that Lizzy felt nothing but gratitude. In fact, after such a tumultuous week without a true confidante or even friendly woman in attendance, Lizzy felt her eyes prick with unexpected moisture.

"Thank you, Mrs. Annesley. I am sure I shall take advantage of your experience." From sheer dislike of returning to her room alone, she added, "Will you be returning directly to the parlor or unpacking up here? Would you like company?"

"I shall return in a few minutes, but I must find Miss Darcy's warmer shawl."

Lizzy followed her into Miss Darcy's larger room, which fronted the street with a fine view of the trees that lined the walk.

A servant was already shaking out Miss Darcy's dresses and hanging them neatly. Mrs. Annesley turned to a trunk and began sifting through it. "Miss Darcy is the dearest girl. Indeed, she is so happy to be accompanying her brother, she has lost her head a little. She declared it the warmest, sunniest day when we left London, but that was more wish than truth, and she has been shivering in the carriage this last half hour."

Lizzy wondered if it was appropriate to say that she looked forward to meeting Miss Darcy? It was true. She found that, in her heart, she believed Darcy's account of Wickham's actions, and that made her both eager and reluctant to meet the girl he had nearly ruined. How could even a very bad man reconcile running away with a naive young girl? Maybe she was as cold and proud as Wickham had said, but no one deserved such a heartless manipulation.

Mrs. Annesley would know all, most likely, but that did not help Lizzy, who would sooner have tied her garter in public than ask about the trials of the young Miss Darcy.

Mrs. Annesley pulled up a lovely blue woolen shawl with triumph.

"Aha!" She rose to her feet with a hand on the edge of the trunk. "Now we can return to the parlor. I daresay they will be calling us for tea soon."

She chatted amiably about Tunbridge as they descended the stairs and Lizzy entered the parlor behind her, thankful for the shield.

Lizzy was largely silent during the teatime, but she discovered several things.

First, that Miss Darcy, though tall and rather square-shouldered for a female, was a sweet, retiring girl. She was as shy as Lydia was bold and couldn't have been further from Wickham's description of her. This proof of false-hood, more than anything, convinced her that Mr. Darcy had been truthful in his account.

Second, Mr. Darcy appeared as impassive as ever, but a slight flush marked his cheeks. Unless he had gotten an un-usual amount of sun in the last few days, she could only attribute it to some discomfort in her presence.

Third, she realized that Lady Catherine was eyeing Lizzy's new, quieter demeanor with an ugly, triumphant gleam in her eye.

This last hit her on the raw. Lizzy had had a trying few days, and she expected more. She was grappling with newly realized faults in her own character, the betrayal of a near friend, and the sneaking fear that she had made a large mistake.

To see Lady Catherine's disdainful smirk was too much.

Lizzy had truly said that her courage rose at every attempt to subdue it. As silence fell over the small group, Lizzy looked up from her teacup. With a deliberate smile and tilt of her head, she said, "Lady Catherine, you did not yet tell Mr. Darcy of the amusing anecdote Lady Mathilde related to you yesterday."

Lizzy had heard this conversation herself though not been part of it, and there was nothing wrong with her comment, but Lady Catherine frowned. No doubt she could hear the new determination in Lizzy's tone.

Lady Catherine related the story, but kept one of her large, protruding eyes on Lizzy. When Lizzy laughed at the story, she frowned again. Lizzy kept her head up and continued to chat amiably with the Colonel with the occasional additions of Mrs. Annesley, who showed herself to be just as kind and well-spoken as Lizzy had thought.

Lizzy did not try to draw Mr. Darcy into the conversation, but when he spoke, she looked directly at him, in an open, friendly way that cost her something to maintain, but hopefully taught Lady Catherine a lesson.

Indeed, was there a slight look of fear in her eyes now? Lizzy hoped so. It would serve the old dragon right to be afraid that her nephew might yet be caught by an un-crushed Lizzy Bennet.

When Colonel Fitzwilliam drew Miss Darcy toward the fire to show him her latest sketches, Anne retired to rest. Lizzy would have left with her—her new determination to stand up to Lady Catherine not overriding her actual du-ties—but Anne shook her head. "I don't want you," she said plainly.

Mrs. Annesley had a slight frown on her forehead at this, but no one else seemed to think much of it. Mr. Darcy remained at the table, and though Lizzy was half tempted to spite Lady Catherine by starting a conversation with him, she was not that confident. The proposal and the letter lay between them.

Instead, she drifted towards the fireside, and hesitated behind Miss Darcy's chair to see her drawings as she leafed through them with the Colonel. Caroline Bingley, who had so desired to have her brother marry Miss Darcy, had praised the young lady to the skies. Seeing her charming and picturesque sketches of everything from a rose to a bee-tle, Lizzy had to admit that in her drawing, at least, Caro-line had not exaggerated Miss Darcy's skills.

Miss Darcy started slightly. "Oh, Miss Bennet. I apolo-gize, I did not see you there."

"Not at all, I should apologize for shamelessly looking over your shoulder. None of my sisters except the eldest are at all artistic, so it is a treat for me."

Miss Darcy blushed. "I would hardly call these a treat, but thank you. I hope you will also play for us sometime, Miss Bennet. My brother says you play delightfully."

Lizzy nearly choked. A muffled noise from the table seemed to indicate that Mr. Darcy had the same problem. Miss Darcy must not realize what had passed between her brother and Miss Bennet; how should she? But how awkward.

Lizzy had always thought Darcy censured her playing, but now even that perception was being turned on its head. The fact that he had praised her to his sister somehow touched her heart in a way his professed affection had not.

Lizzy colored but replied calmly, "I'm afraid I'm not at all above the average, but if you should ever care to try a duet with me, I would be delighted."

Lady Catherine spoke up. "Miss Darcy needs no accompanist. She is accomplished in both the pianoforte and the harp."

"Perhaps you would sing with me," Miss Darcy put in shyly. "I do not have the volume or tone for much display."

Lady Catherine cackled unkindly. "Miss Bennet at least has the volume."

Miss Darcy's face faltered at her aunt's barely veiled insult.

Mrs. Annesley came to the rescue, turning the conversation and inquiring about the plans for the evening.

Lizzy couldn't help glancing at Mr. Darcy and noticing his clenched jaw and even more heightened color. How difficult! Perhaps it would have been best if he'd not returned to Tunbridge with his sister.

{ 11 }

AS DARCY DRESSED FOR DINNER, he cursed his lack of foresight. He had written to his sister from Netherfield and Rosings, and unfortunately, he had written of Elizabeth from both places. He had been at first unconscious of his growing feelings, but even at Netherfield he had praised her quick wit, her well-informed mind, and her care for her sister. From Rosings… well, he did not remember exactly what he had written, but it was written by a man slowly deciding to propose his life and heart to a woman.

It had never occurred to him to tell Georgiana that his suit had failed. He was intensely private, and he still thought of his sister as a little girl in many ways. But now—with her not knowing! She was unconsciously embarrassing him, and perhaps might even seek to encourage Elizabeth! She was a quiet, well-behaved girl, of course, but even a quiet, well-behaved girl could mortify her brother by sharing his former praise with the woman who had rejected him. He had entirely overlooked that possibility and felt a fool.

Just before dinner, he knocked on his sister's door, and she opened it with some surprise. "Yes, brother?"

"Could I have a word?"

Her maid slipped away and shut the door behind her.

"Is something amiss?" Georgiana asked.

"No. But I… I must tell you something. I must ask you not to tell Miss Bennet…that I… That is…"

Georgiana looked really alarmed now, doubtless at his unusual difficulty in stringing a simple sentence together.

"I proposed to Miss Bennet and she declined," Darcy finally said, marshalling his tongue into order. How blunt and humiliating it sounded, stated so.

His sister's expression morphed rapidly from worry to compassion. "Oh, Fitzwilliam!" She rarely used his first name. Her hands fluttered, as though she would embrace him, but she held back. "I am so very sorry."

"Yes, well. There is nothing more to be said on that front. I merely wished to inform you so that you may refrain from repeating to her any ill-judged comments I may have made in my letters."

"I—but—of course," she said, her hands falling to her side and a thoughtful look coming over her. "But, may I ask something?"

Darcy forced a smile. "Of course, Georgiana, you know you may."

"Why are we... here? I would have thought... the last place..." She faded away inarticulately, turning a bright pink.

It was a good question and Darcy felt himself stiffen. "I had told my aunt and the Colonel my plans. I could not change them, then." The half-truth of this sat uneasy with him. "I *would* not change my plans, I should say."

He could not possibly explain to his sister his deeper purpose. His need to save face, and to somehow... inoculate himself against Miss Bennet's charms.

Georgiana did not seem to expect more of him and only nodded quietly.

With that Darcy had to be content, and he escorted her down to dinner.

Lizzy sat near the foot of the table and couldn't help but wonder at the strange assortment of the party. Herself and Mrs. Annesley along with Colonel Fitzwilliam at one end, with Miss de Bourgh, Miss Darcy, Mr. Darcy, and Lady Catherine at the other. The table was not large, but there may as well have been six empty seats between the two parties. Seven was a difficult number to seat well at the best of times.

Lizzy did not mind, but instead exercised her newfound determination to be lively and gay. She and Colonel

Fitzwilliam were as good of friends as ever, and Mrs. Annesley was well-known to Colonel Fitzwilliam, as he was one of Miss Darcy's guardians.

He treated her as perhaps a loved aunt or older sister, and she, while always perfectly deferential and proper, treated him as a much loved but overgrown schoolboy.

Their ease with each other, in fact, made Lizzy feel slightly ashamed. She had indulged some petty resentment at the degradation of becoming a paid companion, but did that mean she would call Mrs. Annesley low or degraded?

All her feelings revolted. Mrs. Annesley was a truly lady-like woman, kind-hearted and elegant. Lizzy would never think less of her for her position. Had Lizzy, in her own disappointed feelings after her father's letter, been just as vain and status-driven as Mr. Darcy? She had certainly resented the situation and her father's mistake quite hotly, despite her sympathy for him.

It was yet another piece of her conduct she could not defend. Was she really defined by vanity? Both in the case of Mr. Wickham's flattery, and in her poor attitude towards her current position, it certainly seemed that pride had dominated.

Lizzy forced these thoughts away, to be examined later.

She also noticed that Miss Darcy was studying her quite intently. Her gaze was much more thoughtful than it had been in the afternoon, at times almost fierce. And when her gaze lit on her brother, it grew downright sorrowful and compassionate. Lizzy was struck with the mortifying thought that Mr. Darcy must have told his sister what passed between them.

Well, Lizzy amended, surely he'd not told her *everything* that passed between them. Probably just the mere fact of his offer and her rejection, but that was still enough to make Lizzy feel self-conscious. Miss Darcy did not seem to realize how clearly she broadcast her dismay.

Happily, Colonel Fitzwilliam did not seem at all conscious, so Lizzy could only assume he was not in his cousin's confidence.

When the ladies retired to the parlor, leaving the two gentlemen to their port, Lizzy moved to a window-seat and was surprised when Lady Catherine called to her. "No, come here Miss Bennet, I wish to have a little dialogue with you." She waved her hand imperiously and the other ladies melted away, clearly used to her autocratic manner.

"Now, Miss Bennet," Lady Catherine began. It was the first time she had spoken in a lowered voice and Lizzy was somewhat amazed it was possible. "I don't know what you mean to be at, after your shocking disclosure to me yesterday. I am still incredulous that my nephew could have acted so. But if you did indeed refuse him, as seems now to be likely, I applaud you."

Lady Catherine's sharp eyes must have understood Miss Darcy's expressive face during dinner as clearly as she had. Lizzy remained silent.

"I would even admit to having been somewhat mistaken in my judgment of your character. I still think it impudent to have flirted with him and then rejected him, but better by far than to have accepted him. You must know that you would never be accepted by his family, which for you would be a humiliation beyond even the pollution of the Pemberley estate and traditions."

Lizzy's cheeks heated with anger, but she also couldn't help glancing around, unsettled that they might be overheard. The other ladies had grouped around the small pianoforte, where Georgiana was playing a few light airs.

"Lady Catherine," Lizzy interrupted, "this conversation is both insulting and improper. It can have no good outcome and, as you have already agreed, is unnecessary. Let us not canvass what can only—"

"How you do interrupt! This is all to say, that having got you out of his system, my nephew will be all the more ready to offer for his true match, Anne. Often young men must have several approaches to matrimony before they see wisdom. It has worked just as I thought."

"Congratulations," Lizzy said shortly. "Would you prefer to dispense with my services now? I can return to London on the Mail."

"No, why? As I say, I've come to the conclusion that he's got this wild idea out of his system, and you have accomplished that. Also, you have too much spirit to make any of us uncomfortable, I will say that for you. Indeed, I'd already decided that you may stay, as a salutary reminder to him."

Lizzy stood abruptly, incensed, but before she could stalk away, the gentlemen entered the room.

Caught unexpected, and in turmoil, Lizzy looked right in Mr. Darcy's eyes. She saw there his immediate heartfelt response to the distress that must be on her face. His expression softened, his lips parted, but then he recalled himself.

He looked away. Lizzy got herself under control. The group shifted, cutting through the cord that seemed to have momentarily connected them.

Lizzy retired to the window seat and was thankful that only placid Mrs. Annesley joined her. That lady seemed to sense that Lizzy was upset, and provided a calm, undemanding presence that soothed her.

Would Lady Catherine never cease to surprise her? She was vulgar and demanding and self-centered, but perhaps it was for the best that she had shared her thoughts with Lizzy. At least Lizzy didn't have to guess whether she would be peremptorily dispatched anytime soon.

Yes, perhaps it was for the best that Miss Darcy had such an unguarded face. Lizzy could be relatively certain that Lady Catherine would not broach the matter with Mr. Darcy.

With this and that, she managed to get through the evening and could only hope her riotous emotions would be lessened in the morning.

{ 12 }

AFTER BREAKFAST, DARCY WENT around to the stables to request the carriage. Lady Catherine had expressed a desire to see the nearby abbey ruin and had insisted they make a party of it. A carriage for the ladies and horses for the gentlemen.

She'd insisted, even though Anne had looked particularly sick after returning from the pump room this morning. Even Darcy had noted it. He'd mentioned it to Lady Catherine, adding that his cousin might not wish for a fatiguing day trip. That piece of kindness had backfired spectacularly, though.

Lady Catherine had smiled triumphantly. "I am pleased to see how your thoughtfulness for Anne grows daily, but she will be fine. She improves every day."

There was no doubt that Lady Catherine was referring to her settled idea that Darcy should marry Anne someday.

He had tried over the years since he reached his majority to quietly show that this was not to be, but she persisted.

As he walked back from the stables, he encountered Chuff. His friend greeted him with all his usual cheer, telling him how much his wife had enjoyed their dinner party. He swung a cane. "I must have you all over again. Indeed, I shall, if your aunt will spare another evening. Honoria needs cheering up. That's a dashed nice gal who's staying with your cousin."

Darcy murmured an indifferent assent. Chuff bumped him. "Really, man, you made a very nice picture, you and her and the babe she was holding. Could have imagined it was yours."

Darcy made a face. Had he been so indiscreet? Would he be forced to tell *everyone* of his rejected suit?

But Chuff moved on, satisfied with his teasing, and Darcy returned to the hotel alone, dreading the coming outing.

The ladies were eventually ready to leave, properly hatted, gloved, and shawled for the expedition. One would think it February rather than a blessedly dry day in April.

Darcy was surprised, as they toured the ruins, to see that Elizabeth seemed to be seeking a chance to speak to him. He obligingly dropped back, considering a mossy gravestone with the unlikely surname of Daft.

She kept her eyes on the gravestone as well. "Mr. Darcy, I wished to apologize as soon as I could, for unfavorably judging you on Mr. Wickham's testimony. It was—not very Christian of me."

His eyes tried to find her profile, though her face was partially blocked by the bonnet. "Thank you. I also apologize if I erred in judging your sister's affection."

She nodded. Her eyes finally rose to his, and she looked adorably perplexed. "I find I truly do not understand your character."

Darcy felt an unwelcome surge of hope. "Perhaps you can judge more clearly, now that no one is actively disparaging me."

"But it was not only that—" She broke off, and the bonnet tilted down again.

"Not only that?"

"Excuse me. I will rejoin the party."

"No, come now," Darcy said, somewhat desperately though his voice only grew sterner. "You cannot say something like that and walk away."

"Surely I can, if I shall thereby avoid rudeness. You must allow me to swallow back comments I think better of. *You* may have iron control of your tongue, but I confess I do not."

She walked determinedly on, and Darcy followed. "Can you not complete your thought in a way that does justice to your scruples? If not, that certainly reflects poorly on me."

"You have neatly trapped me, sir. If I speak I shall give offense, and if I don't, you're determined to take it in the worst way."

He reached for her arm, to pause her. "I'm not so quick to take offense at an honest rebuke. I would always rather a man speak plainly with me than otherwise."

Her mouth compressed. "I was determined to apologize and say nothing else, but you are determined to exasperate me. Very well then. It was not merely Wickham's... lies that influenced me. Your whole manner during your time in Hertfordshire was calculated to offend. You would not stoop to dance, unless forced. You would not stoop to conversation, unless it were with your party. You were most unguarded in your expressions of distaste and even disgust. That does not argue an amiable temper or... or even the common manners of a gentleman."

Darcy rocked back on his heels as though struck.

"You did insist, Mr. Darcy."

Several angry retorts sprang to mind, regarding the inanity and sometimes downright vulgarity of those occasions, but Mr. Darcy, who did indeed have something like iron control over his tongue, did not utter them.

She must have seen the emotion in his eyes, however, for she responded. "I believe you when you say you prefer plain-speaking from a man, but perhaps that does not extend to your female acquaintance. Do excuse me."

She continued on and Darcy allowed her to outpace him.

Lizzy hurried to catch up with the others, her mind a perfect whirlwind. Regret, satisfaction, and decorum all battled in her heart over her blunt speech, but on the whole, she was not sorry to have told him the truth.

Mr. Darcy circled the other way around the remains of the abbey, only one wall of which stood more than waist-high, and eventually joined the group from the other direction. Lady Catherine commanded him to escort the young ladies, by which she meant Anne and Georgiana, to a sunny slope nearby, where "they might sketch the scene." There was no consciousness or anger in her voice, so Lizzy dared to hope that Lady Catherine had missed their tête-à-tête.

Lizzy and Mrs. Annesley trailed behind the trio.

"I don't think that Miss de Bourgh is feeling at all well today," Mrs. Annesley said. "Look there, she is tripping again."

"She does indeed look pale and uncomfortable," Lizzy agreed, thankful to have Mr. Darcy far ahead so that she could recover her composure. "But I—I honestly do not know what to do to help her. She does not like me and whenever I try to help, she generally rejects it at once."

Mrs. Annesley's brow furrowed. "I admit that I have suspected as much. It is most odd that—" She broke off, coloring faintly. "Forgive me, my dear."

"Most odd that Lady Catherine should choose me? You need not scruple to say so." Lizzy's face heated, thinking of the true reason she'd been asked. She continued, "Lady Catherine definitely seems to have changed her approach to Miss de Bourgh's delicacy."

"We probably ought not discuss it," Mrs. Annesley said mildly. "It is best not to be too inquisitive as a companion."

"I have no objection and would much rather talk of other things. Do you know if you and Miss Darcy make a long stay in Tunbridge? Have you been here before?"

They spoke of indifferent things, but when they caught up with the party, Lizzy wasn't sure what to do. Georgiana sat perched on a rock, sketch book in her lap, and her pencil flying across it. A pleased, absorbed focus seemed to separate her from the rest of the group. Mrs. Annesley moved to stand behind her, quietly watching. Anne leaned on Mr. Darcy's arm, looking as pinched and unapproachable as ever.

Lizzy ought probably to hover near Miss de Bourgh, as Mrs. Annesley was doing with her charge, but that would mean hovering near Mr. Darcy, and that was not to be borne.

Lizzy stood alone, admiring the view, or attempting to admire it. She would always rather be walking when agitated, and to stand still and listen to the desultory conversation between Mr. Darcy and Miss de Bourgh left her itching to be away.

Eventually, Georgiana slowed in her drawing, taking time to look to and from her paper to the slight valley below her.

A fitful wind caught the page and swept it right out of her book. Darcy took a single stride toward it, but it fluttered past Lizzy, who ran it down in a few seconds. She smoothed it against her skirt and walked it back to Georgiana.

"Oh, thank you. It was careless of me to keep a loose sheet in here." Georgiana's face was somehow almost childlike in its expressions. Her face brightened happily but then closed and darkened when another thought obtruded. "Thank you."

"No harm done, I think," Lizzy added.

Georgiana accepted the paper back silently and tucked it into the back of her book.

"Will you start another?" Lizzy asked.

Georgiana looked unsure and Mr. Darcy spoke up. "I think not today, Georgiana. Our cousin is fatigued and ready to return to the carriage."

"Of course, brother." Georgiana sprang up, shaking out her skirt and tucking her sketch book under her arm. "I apologize for keeping all of you."

Lizzy walked next to Mrs. Annesley again as they made their way back, and that woman looked uncommonly thoughtful.

"Miss Bennet, am I correct that you were previously acquainted with Mr. Darcy?"

"Why, yes, a little," Lizzy faltered. How did one describe such an uneven and confusing acquaintanceship?

"Did you... perhaps have a disagreeable conversation with him today? I don't ask for vulgar curiosity sake, you understand, only that I have known him for years and never saw him look quite as he did just now. I would hate for any misunderstanding or quarrel to... to mar this pleasant visit."

"If I am perfectly honest, yes. I may have spoken a little... critically to him. Though he did ask my opinion on his behavior, which was the topic." What a strange conversation to have! Lizzy's natural good humor began to return at the very absurdity of it.

"Criticize Mr. Darcy's behavior?" Mrs. Annesley sounded scandalized. "How could you?"

"I recognize that as a companion it is not at all the thing to have an opinion. I assure you I shall try to have as little conversation with him as possible, going forward."

"I did not mean it in that way. It is that Mr. Darcy is such a good, generous, kind-hearted gentleman. I cannot imagine finding fault with him."

Lizzy couldn't help a smile. "But may that not have more to do with your own good disposition than his? Or his sister's praise of him?"

"She adores him, of course. But I have been acquainted with him all his life, for my mother was connected with the family. I have seen him grow from a stout, good-natured boy to a fine man. When I think of what others have grown to be…" She trailed off with a dark look.

Was she speaking of Wickham? Lizzy longed to ask, but they were nearly back to the carriage and so she had to give it up. The next time opportunity offered, Lizzy was determined to get more information from Mrs. Annesley.

{ 13 }

THAT AFTERNOON, LIZZY SAT unobtrusively in the corner of the parlor, her back to the window. Ostensibly, she was reading, but while she loved to read, she could not say that it was keeping her attention from the conversation around her.

The men had gone out and Anne was resting in her room, but Lady Catherine was still full of energy after their little jaunt and was receiving callers. She clearly enjoyed it excessively.

Lizzy was amazed the grand lady could stand so many months sequestered at Rosings. No wonder she had the Collinses every week!

Most of the other ladies were also matrons of Lady Catherine's generation, though a few sons and daughters were present as well. These younger ones tended to drift toward Miss Darcy, though she was significantly younger than even them.

Her manners were everything to be expected from a young woman of quality, but she was shy, and her shyness rendered her stiff. If Lizzy had not seen her interact with her brother and family in the past two days and had only this moment to judge her, Lizzy would think her every bit as arrogant and stuffy as Wickham had described.

As it was, she instead saw a young woman beset merely by uncertainty. Lizzy had tried, twice, to join the conversations around her to help Miss Darcy on, but that had merely increased the poor girl's discomfort and rendered her nearly incapable of speech.

Lizzy found herself regretting that the first evening—when Miss Darcy still thought Lizzy in her brother's favor—was the last time Lizzy would see that version of the girl.

Lizzy did not join the conversation again until Lady Honoria entered the parlor. She was escorted by her maid, who moved off immediately, probably to join the other maids in the common parlor. Seats were not in abundance, with so many, but Lady Honoria did not look sorry to join Lizzy in the window seat.

"What a crush," she said genially. "Lady Catherine can always command a crowd."

"Indeed."

"And you have chosen the best spot, whereby to watch them all."

"Guilty," Lizzy admitted with a smile. She felt some awkwardness when conversing with any member (however remote!) of Darcy's family, but she was not averse to talking if Lady Honoria wished it. "Are you acquainted with most of these ladies, ma'am?"

"Oh, lord, yes. Acquainted, that is, none of them are my close friends. Mrs. Winkleigh, now," Lady Honoria nodded to one middle-aged matron, "she is calculating when Miss Darcy will be presented, and wondering whether her son will be down from Oxford during Miss Darcy's first season. Her son aspires to be quite the scholar, I do believe, and she is in anxiety over it." Lady Honoria favored her with some more pithy descriptions of the present company, and Lizzy laughed.

The lady smiled appreciatively. "Now, you, I do not know much about, other than that you hail from Hertfordshire. Do enlighten me."

Lizzy spread her hands, "I'm afraid I am not so interesting. My father owns a moderate estate near Meryton, and I am the second of his five daughters. Our estate is entailed on a cousin, Mr. Collins, who is the rector of the Hunsford Parish. That is how I became acquainted with Lady Catherine."

Lady Honoria looked very arch. "And how did you become so well-acquainted with my cousin Darcy?"

Lizzy blushed uncomfortably. Did no one in Mr. Darcy's family have any reserve? Had he absorbed all the rigidness of the family and left none for them?

She was spared a response. Lady Honoria touched her arm. "No need to stiffen up. I won't press you. I will only say that I pride myself on being an excellent observer of persons, and I have taken a fancy to you."

"You're kind, Lady Honoria. I assure you it is mutual! Although I cannot claim to be such an acute observer as you. I used to pride myself on being an excellent judge of character, but I have recently had my eyes opened to my folly. So now I must take your good judgment on faith."

She laughed. "Oh, you may, I have confidence enough for the both of us. Too much, my husband would tell you."

"Surely not."

"No, I suppose not. Charles has the sweetest of dispositions and is generally happy to do whatever I prefer."

"A paragon of a husband!"

"Indeed." She smiled drolly. "But that is not to say that a more decisive husband would be less so. There is something quite appealing about a man who takes charge."

Lizzy again felt the discomfort of the implied subject and turned it away with nonsense. "Of course! I should much prefer a dictatorial sort of man – one who would tell me what to wear and what to eat and what to read. Imagine the time I should save in planning and choosing and dressing! And if I am lucky, he will be a loud and blustery man, as well. All the better to know his mood; I shall never be in doubt of his true feelings."

Lady Honoria smiled knowingly at this sally, and Lizzy wondered if she'd inadvertently given something away.

"And how are your beautiful twins doing today?" Lizzy asked abruptly.

Lady Honoria was too natural a mother to resist this temptation, and so she favored Lizzy with an account of their many trials.

When several of the other guests took their leave, temporarily leaving Miss Darcy alone, Lady Honoria turned to her. "Cousin Georgiana, I hear you are recently escaped from your establishment in Ramsgate. Did you enjoy it there?"

Lizzy was certain Lady Honoria meant this in a completely innocent fashion, but Georgiana paled and then flushed as if she'd been slapped.

"I did not particularly—I preferred the ladies' seminary..." Miss Darcy trailed off inarticulately.

"I'm afraid I did not have the benefit of any masters in my own education," Lizzy broke in, kindly. "I always had my father's library, but for the arts, we girls were rather on our own. How long were you at your school?"

With this concrete, unexceptionable question, Miss Darcy recovered her tongue and managed a faint answer. She still did not look Lizzy in the face, but between them,

Lizzy and Lady Honoria managed a cheerful conversation with her.

When the time for calls was over, Lady Honoria took her leave, and Miss Darcy immediately moved away from Lizzy.

{ 14 }

IN THE EVENING, WHEN LIZZY found herself again sequestered in the window-seat, but with Mrs. Annesley this time, she ventured on a little fact-finding. The gentlemen were out and Georgiana played piano.

It was not hard to get the good lady to mention Pemberley and from there to describe its relative situation in the countryside and the beauty of its grounds.

"I made an acquaintance in the militia who also spoke of Pemberley with great fondness," Lizzy said. "A Mr. Wickham. I believe he mentioned his father was the caretaker."

Mrs. Annesley's jaw clenched and her mouth thinned. "That young man is a… a *louse*."

Lizzy raised her eyebrows. "I am sorry. I did not mean to upset you. I was not well-acquainted with him." Which was no more than the truth. She'd thought she knew him quite well, but obviously not at all.

"Of course not. You would not know. It is not my place to share all his *crimes*… but a more nasty, unthankful, greedy young man…! Oh, I cannot talk about him in moderation. He ought to be run out of the country."

There was nothing to do but apologize and move on from the conversation, but Elizabeth had all the confirmation she needed. The way Mrs. Annesley's eyes lingered on Georgiana, filled with a mix of sorrow and anger, Lizzy had no doubt the attempted elopement was the source of her ferocity.

And perhaps Miss Darcy would have continued to keep her distance from Lizzy for the remainder of her visit, but for a most unfortunate happening. Mrs. Annesley, going down the stairs early the next morning, slipped on a bit of muck that someone must have carelessly tracked in. She slid down four stairs, collided with a maid at the bottom, and was found, after it all, to have a severely sprained ankle.

"It is the most mortifying circumstance," she told Lizzy, whom she'd requested to come to her after the physician left. "I have never done such a clumsy thing in my life, Miss Bennet! To have faltered here, when Miss Darcy is not even in her own home—!"

Lizzy had never seen the placid companion so frustrated.

"And I know I ought not repine overly—accidents *do* happen, heaven knows—but the inconvenience to Miss Darcy and Mr. Darcy makes me very unhappy."

"I am sure they only wish you to rest and recover," Lizzy offered. "And in a few days, you can travel in a coach, so it is not as if you are keeping them here. I am sure the inconvenience is minimal, ma'am."

"Perhaps I have allowed myself to be overly agitated. But I must ask that you will make an effort to… to extend your duties to Miss Darcy for at least the next few days. A girl in her circumstances… she cannot be too cautious."

"I understand, but I am not sure they want me—"

"No, no, I've spoken to Mr. Darcy already, and he quite agreed that you are an unexceptionable person to help chaperone her while I am laid up."

"It is all settled then," Lizzy declared. "And you've nothing to do but put your foot back up on that pillow— yes, I heard the doctor tell you so!—and rest, ma'am. Please do not worry."

And although Miss Darcy would rather have stayed in her room for a week than go on any outings with Miss Bennet, her aunt would not allow her to miss the daily visits to the bath house. There, the three girls—Anne, Georgiana, and Lizzy—sat on the stiff couches facing one another while Miss de Bourgh sullenly tried to drink an exorbitant amount of water.

Lizzy would sometimes try to fill the silence to amuse or at least distract either young lady, but neither gave her much encouragement. Anne, because she despised her; Georgiana, because she resented her. Or perhaps *resentment* was too strong a word for Georgiana's gentle nature. Say rather that she had an air of injured confusion around Lizzy which could not be penetrated.

Lizzy's self-consciousness with the younger girl (and even Mr. Darcy) had nearly worn itself out by the end of the week. Yes, it was an awkward situation, but proposals were made and refused every day! It was not a murder.

When Lady Catherine compelled Mr. Darcy to escort Anne back to the hotel one morning, adding carelessly, "Miss Eliza, do escort Miss Darcy when she is finished speaking with Major Trenton," Lizzy was a little glad. She caught Miss Darcy's startled and unhappy look, but the poor girl was too polite to abruptly end her conversation with the aged military man.

He monopolized her with talk of her father and grandfather and their mutual friends for a good half hour before his crony came to take him away.

Miss Darcy expelled a long breath, and Lizzy nodded. "A most estimable gentleman but clearly he forgot you weren't old enough to know the half of those persons."

Miss Darcy rose from the settee. "It's true. Even my father, I barely… It's my brother who r-reared me, you see." She looked self-conscious and shut her lips firmly.

Miss Darcy paused near the windows. The little boy in fancy clothes, his ruffled shirt quite high around his neck, was back on the picturesque lounge with his mother. He squirmed in his small jacket and scratched his knee. The painter and easel were set up as before for the portraitist.

Georgiana looked back and forth, comparing the painting with what she saw before her.

"You like art, Miss Darcy?"

"Oh yes! Though I shouldn't know how to attempt anything so ambitious."

Miss Darcy seemed absorbed in the process. Elizabeth supposed the canvas was rather large; probably the size was commissioned by the fond mama who was currently urging her darling to sit still, but Lizzy didn't know enough of art to be otherwise impressed. Most of the canvas was filled with a fine painting of the bath house, though more colorful than what she saw here. The son and mother had been sketched in, and the painter was now filling in their faces.

"I'm afraid the faces do not look very like the subjects," Lizzy commented to Miss Darcy. "Your sketches seem more accurate to me, but perhaps that is intentional."

"Oh no, they will be excellent. He is only completing the underpainting now, the values of the light and shadow on their faces. It will look quite different when more color is added. And see how he has positioned them just so? Not in profile and not full on—there is nothing so difficult as a child's smooth face."

The painter, just in front of them, turned his head slightly. "Well put, ma'am."

Miss Darcy stepped further back.

"Oh, forgive us. We did not mean to interrupt you," Lizzy said.

"Not at all," he said politely, facing toward the canvas. "I would say that I hope you will come to judge my progress another day, but there is no one to perform an introduction, so I suppose I cannot."

Lizzy laughed, but it was true that it was hardly proper to talk to a man they had not been properly introduced to, one moreover, who was working, so she merely wished him a good day and escorted Miss Darcy out.

That young lady, whether from embarrassment at being overheard, or perhaps merely from being left alone with Lizzy, retreated to intense silence as they took the wide, shallow stairs that led down to the street.

"Please, Miss Darcy, may I be frank?" Lizzy asked. "We are awkwardly placed here, but we are stuck with each other for the moment. Could we not be friends, or at least amiable acquaintances, in the interim? I assure you I am not the heartless minx you seem to think me."

Miss Darcy was wholly unused to such plain-speaking. She stumbled through several half-sentences, but Lizzy, while feeling for her, tried again. Despite Miss Darcy's shyness and youth, she possessed a good understanding. Lizzy felt that, if not for current circumstances, they could have been friends. "I only ask, Miss Darcy, that you reserve judgment on me as you would any acquaintance, that had made... perhaps a mistake. A mistake in manners, I mean, that perhaps injured someone you care about. You would not be implacably set against such a person, would you?"

"No, of course not. Forgiveness is... well, I should try..."

"Exactly, you would try to overlook the offense."

Miss Darcy pursed her lips even more firmly together. Finally she spoke, almost in a whisper, but as if compelled for someone else's sake, "Do you mean that... rejecting him was a mistake?"

Lizzy's eyes widened. She could not allow this to reach Mr. Darcy. "The *manner* in which I rejected him, that I regret most heartily. However, I still believe we should not...suit. For his future happiness as much as my own, I must adhere to that answer."

"But he is not happy," Georgiana truly whispered now.

"Perhaps not... but believe me, he is far happier than he should be with such a woman as me. I would complicate his life in a thousand ways," Lizzy answered lightly.

"Oh no," Georgiana answered. "No one can solve problems like him; he simply slices through complications."

Lizzy imagined his money had much to do with that, but figured saying so *would* take plain-speaking too far. "Be that as it may, I hope you and I can be more at ease with one another."

When the conversation moved back from her brother to her, Georgiana grew uncomfortable again. It seemed only her brother's interest could bring out that bold side of her.

Lizzy sighed. Perhaps some progress had been made, though it was hard to tell.

And why was she so disappointed to fail to win over Miss Darcy? Lizzy was never one to repine overly about another's opinion. As she pictured what she wanted, a pleasant mental image of their party formed itself in her mind's eye. Miss de Bourgh would be well and warm by the fire, Georgiana would be smiling and happy, and Mr. Darcy looking on benevolently... Lizzy realized with a start that it was *his* reaction she most wanted.

Good heavens, when did she begin to want his good opinion so much? Was it just to show him that she regretted what she'd said about Wickham, and she truly cared about his sister's recovery? Or what was it?

He had been most stoic since their conversation at the abbey. He barely opened his mouth and when he did he never spoke to her. His face had gone back to the forbidding aspect it generally wore in Hertfordshire, and only now, in comparison, did she realize how much he had relaxed before his proposal.

She wanted... She wanted him to be *that* version of himself again.

And why? her interrogation continued.

Because then she would know she hadn't made a mistake.

Lizzy nearly gasped at her own revelation. In her heart of hearts, she *was* afraid that perhaps she should have accepted him. She was afraid that perhaps the good-humored Darcy, the warm, talking one, would have been an excellent match for her. His manners were not so good, but could he not learn better, when such good material occasionally peeked through from within? His disposition was not generally pleasing, but then, his understanding was superior and perhaps they could each have benefitted...

But what was the good in such musings? She had rejected him.

Lizzy ended the walk just as tongue-tied as poor Miss Darcy.

{ 15 }

DARCY RODE OUT OF TUNBRIDGE alone that morning, desperate to get out of the stifling hotel. He
put his horse down the post road, but when a
broad, gently rising field presented itself on the right, with
only a short fence to jump, he turned off the road immediately. What he needed was a gallop.

The Kentish countryside was abloom with spring. The
trees along the road wore their brightest green of fresh
leaves, and the turf that squelched up under his horse's
hooves was heavy with fresh rain and thick clay. The High
Weald was much admired for its beauty, though the soil
was not much good for crops, being too clay-like and min-
eral-laden.

He missed Pemberley.

Darcy was being a bad guest; he knew it. He certainly
didn't need Colonel Fitzwilliam's ribbing to bring it to his
attention.

Darcy was being unsociable and even rude on occasion to family, friends, and acquaintances alike. But he was fighting a mental battle, and sometimes twenty minutes passed before he realized that he'd stopped engaging with the people around him. He was not quick to laugh at jokes when he was fighting with his own disappointment, and he was not a good conversationalist when he was not in the mood.

Worse, he was honest enough to recognize that his current behavior was almost exactly what it had been in Hertfordshire, though for different reasons.

While there, he had barely considered what his behavior *ought* to be, he had been wholly distracted by the vulgarity of everyone *else's* behavior. He had been just as rude and disconnected, but he had not cared, even when Bingley brought it to his attention.

His old defense reared its head to protest: Why should he care what they thought: a set of people so far below him?

But then his finer instincts would roar back in. So far *below* you? Is rank and fortune all that matters in such circles?

Did he believe in decency and courtesy only for the *worthy?* Such an attitude said far more about his breeding than theirs.

How ungentlemanly! Darcy spurred his horse at the next fence.

The word rang in his head and faced him in the mirror every morning. He, who had been taught from the cradle to think highly of himself and his breeding, had been called *ungentlemanly!* And it had been true.

The same could be said of the way he had proposed to Miss Elizabeth, though she had not used the word then.

His parents had good morals; they were excellent people. But they had taught him, by their example, to think the name Darcy was above every other name. They had taught him that selfishness was proper pride, and that such pride was only realism. They had taught him to think less even of those he *cared* for, and he had done it to Elizabeth and felt magnanimous about it.

Why should she want to ally herself with a man who put down not just her family but her entire society from birth until this time?

Darcy was not satisfied when he finally turned his horse back the way he had come, but at least he had used some of his pent-up energy. This idle life was not for him.

When he joined the post-road again, he found himself temporarily stuck behind a gentleman's carriage. It looked familiar, in fact, and with a suppressed oath, he recognized the driver as none other than Bingley's coachman, William.

Was Bingley coming to Tunbridge Wells? Why?

Darcy had spent only a single night in London before returning with his sister, and he had not had time, or perhaps sufficient inclination, to seek out his friend to make an embarrassing apology. He knew he ought to say something to Bingley, but what exactly it was, Darcy wasn't certain.

He'd thought to write to his friend, but that seemed to grant more gravity to the situation than was appropriate. Darcy's mouth twisted unhappily as he realized he'd hoped to find an offhand way to make things right with Bingley. A way that avoided a humiliating confession.

He'd hoped the next time he saw Bingley he might merely mention that he may have been mistaken about Miss Jane Bennet's feelings. That Miss Elizabeth said something about her sister's low spirits, despite her visit to London. That would have been plenty to send Bingley around to Jane's lodging with her aunt and uncle.

But now Bingley was here. It served Darcy right for shirking his duty.

Darcy passed the carriage with a nod and brief hello to William. He passed on quickly to return his horse to the stable. He was just returning to the hotel when the Bingleys arrived.

Most of Darcy's questions were answered when the door opened. Bingley sprang out with a cheerful greeting to him and then handed down his sister Caroline.

She smiled widely. "Good morning, Mr. Darcy. I thought I saw you on the road just past. How do you do?"

He took her hand politely.

Miss Bingley squeezed it. "Charles told me you and Georgiana would probably return straight from the Wells to Pemberley, with only a night in London, and I couldn't *bear* not to see her again before you return north."

"That's kind of you," Darcy said automatically.

"But of course! I quite expected you to head home several weeks ago. I was surprised when Charles told me you were both fixed here."

She continued into the hotel, and Darcy directed a maid to escort her to Lady Catherine's parlor where she would no doubt find the ladies of the party at this time. She hesitated for a moment but then followed the maid.

Bingley fell back with him. "No doubt you're surprised to see me. We're only staying a night or two. Caroline wouldn't take no for an answer."

"But did you—" Darcy cut himself off. He wanted to ask if Bingley knew that Elizabeth was here; if Bingley felt composed at the idea of meeting her. But Darcy was a proper English gentleman and as such, did not generally ask his friends about their feelings. Besides, Darcy had shirked his duty long enough.

"Bingley, perhaps Caroline mentioned that Miss Elizabeth Bennet is here. I must tell you that in speaking with her, I realize that I may have made a hasty judgment last fall when you left Netherfield. Miss Elizabeth has mentioned, more than once, that her sister has been in low spirits since you left. She is staying with her aunt and uncle in London."

"Low-spirits? For me?" Mr. Bingley's face opened excitedly. Then he took in the rest of Darcy's explanation and his face closed down. "But... in London, you say? Why would she not call on us? Or at least write to let us know of her visit? But, no, of course she could not write to *me,* but to Caroline...?"

"She called on Caroline, and Caroline returned the visit last month."

"Caroline... concealed it?" Bingley looked a little lost, as only someone so innocent of the dark side of human nature could be. He was not a stupid man, but he would not naturally suspect someone of deception.

"I am afraid I neglected to tell you as well," Darcy admitted.

"But that was unkind."

Darcy shifted uncomfortably. "I do apologize. There was a level of artifice, of passive deception... I was a poor friend. Please forgive me."

Bingley studied the mud on his Hessians. "It was not well done of you, but I suppose I understand your motive."

"Yes, well, I still cannot feel that Miss Bennet's connections are ideal, but that is no excuse for my behavior. I'm sorry."

Bingley's lowered brow and frown slowly gave way to bemusement. "Zounds, Darcy, that's your third apology in as many minutes. It's unnerving. Are you ill?"

"Are you never serious?"

"Of course I am. I might even be angry, but I shall have to consider. You did not actually slander me to Miss Bennet, or anything of that nature, did you?"

"Of course not."

"Well, then I shall ponder what you've said. I imagine I must greet Lady Catherine before long or risk being shockingly ill-behaved."

Darcy thankfully accepted his friend's closing of the uncomfortable conversation.

{ 16 }

LIZZY WAS NOT BEST PLEASED to see Caroline Bingley again and to say that this was reciprocated was a gross understatement. But Caroline at least had the advantage of knowing what she was walking into. Lizzy was taken by surprise at her entrance. Caroline had barely removed her hat and gloves and decently greeted Lady Catherine before she managed to cast a languid and supercilious eye toward Lizzy and greet her with under-handed compliments. Her smile was pure frost, and some-how she managed to mention officers, high spirits, and Mrs. Bennet's nerves in her polite enquiries about the Ben-net family.

Frustratingly, there was not much to say, especially since Lizzy had just received a much-jumbled letter from Lydia in raptures about the officer's ball, which she had been escorted to by some flighty young matron named Mrs. Forster, because Mrs. Bennet's nerves were not well.

Georgiana entered directly and Caroline turned her shoulder to Lizzy, quite clearly dismissing her as a paid servant, and even turned her chair—in the act of warming herself—such as to completely exclude Lizzy from the family circle.

Lizzy was unsurprised at this but could not help the surge of disdain she felt. In another woman, Lizzy might laugh at such blatant snobbery, but Caroline's influence was no doubt the root of Jane's disappointment and that precluded much humor. Lizzy was only surprised that Miss Darcy should look conscious, and even rather guilty, when she observed the snub.

Lizzy was better prepared when Mr. Bingley and Mr. Darcy entered the parlor. Mr. Darcy sat down by his sister, but Bingley immediately put out his hand to Lizzy.

She wasn't quite sure what to expect of him, not knowing whether any of her words had reached him through Mr. Darcy. She expected him, at any rate, to behave with the same warmth and friendliness he had shown her before, because she judged him incapable of anything else. In the event, she was proved right. He greeted her with every sign of pleasure, asking with real warmth about her family, her winter in Hertfordshire, and all their friends there.

Lizzy could not very well probe the heart of the matter in such a setting, but she was determined to judge as best she might by his looks and words the state of his heart. As it was, he surprised her very much by stating nearly right away that he looked forward to seeing Miss Bennet in London. Indeed, "through some great mischance" he had not realized she was already settled there until very recently. A quick, unconscious flick of his eyes toward Darcy told her more than she'd expected.

"I—I am sure she would be pleased to see you there. And Miss Bingley again, of course," Lizzy replied. His lack of surprise confirmed her suspicion that either Darcy or Caroline had made a clean breast of things. Mr. Bingley's lips thinned noticeably, making him look almost fierce for such a sunny-tempered gentleman. Miss Bingley's only acknowledgement was to raise her chin to an even more aristocratic angle as she listened to Lady Catherine's description of Anne's improved health.

Lady Catherine called Bingley over to their group, and with a smile and nod at Lizzy, he obeyed. He traded places with Mr. Darcy, settling on the settee next to Miss Darcy.

Mr. Darcy stepped away to look out the window, which also put him only a pace or two from Lizzy. What did the man want now? Her thanks? Her forgiveness?

Lizzy found herself quite at a loss. Mr. Darcy turned half-towards her as if to speak, but then shut his mouth firmly, as if thinking better of it.

She tried to offer an olive branch. "I hope Miss Darcy will be pleased to see her friend again."

"Yes, of course." He swallowed and quietly added, under his aunt's voice, "I regret that I never apologized for my role in keeping Charles in ignorance of your sister's visit. It was badly done."

"Please, Mr. Darcy, you owe *me* no apology. To Jane, perhaps yes, but it seems that you have made restitution, and Jane is far too forgiving to hold anything against anyone."

He inclined his head but didn't pursue the conversation further.

Lizzy found, to her intense amusement, that Lady Catherine developed an immediate and fierce aversion to Caroline Bingley. It seems that they had not met previously, though Lady Catherine was aware of the friendship. But upon meeting Miss Bingley, she recognized a serious threat.

It began with an interrogation, one that Lizzy herself had undergone only a few months past. Did Miss Bingley play? Why, yes, she was a lover of the art; perhaps she and Miss Darcy "might put on a small concert" that evening. Did Miss Bingley draw? Why, yes, though watercolor was her preferred medium, and she could not compare herself to Miss Darcy. This brought an allusion to how much Mr. Bingley admired Miss Darcy's art. At both of these things, Lady Catherine frowned ominously.

The old lady was no fool, and she seemed to immediately gather the gist of Caroline's schemes: that Bingley and Georgiana might make a match, and ultimately, Caroline and Darcy.

The interrogation continued. Languages? French and Italian, the languages of opera and verse. Connections? Here Miss Bingley, though smoothly spoken as ever, did have a slight hesitation. Her connections were not high, and though her brother was a well-heeled gentleman, they had no family seat as yet and few high connections. She mentioned that her brother was looking to buy a country estate, which made him speak up, confirming his interest in Hertfordshire, with a quick, conscious glance at Lizzy.

Mr. Bingley might have saved his breath; he was not attended to.

Lady Catherine spoke of the longevity of the de Bourgh and Darcy family holdings.

Caroline's eyes narrowed.

Miss Darcy shifted uncomfortably.

It was forming up to be a right battle of wills and it was as good as a play.

Lizzy, who had not much occasion for laughter lately, schooled her face but may perhaps have given away some amusement by the crinkling of her eyes or the dimple that would creep into her cheek even as she suppressed a smile.

Mr. Darcy was studiously not looking at her, but Mr. Bingley, as innocent of the undercurrents as a babe in the sea, smiled at her widely. He had no idea what should make her look so cheerful, and indeed, rather like her sister, but he smiled when he saw something pleasing and did not question it too far. Lizzy smiled back at him, forgiving him even now for his part in hurting Jane. If he and Jane ever resumed their relationship and married, they would be the sweetest, most naïve couple in the country.

{ 17 }

M R. BINGLEY WAS INTERESTED in the local races running at Ashford. He wanted to induce Mr. Darcy and Colonel Fitzwilliam to accompany him there for the rest of the day, enjoying the pleasures of turf and horseflesh rather than hearth and tea, but this did not find favor with either Lady Catherine or Caroline.

Neither lady said exactly that, but by judicious exclamation and comment, as of two dogs tugging on either end of a rope, this neat plan was politely ravaged. It ended that the carriage should be sent for, that Miss Darcy and Miss de Bourgh and Miss Bingley might enjoy the races as well.

Mr. Darcy looked a bit forbidding at this. "She is too young," he said, though not unkindly. "I'll take you another time, my dear."

Georgiana, alive to his disapproval, disclaimed any desire to attend. "Oh, yes! Perhaps we might attend the

Chesterfield races when we are back home, as we once did with Papa and Mama." They both smiled at this recollection, but the affectionate interval was broken off.

Caroline could not bear for her friend to be left out of the treat. "It is not as if we are going to Newmarket, after all! We *can't* forgo Georgiana's company, can we?"

Lady Catherine unexpectedly supported this. Adding that if she judged it not too fast for Anne, Darcy could hardly object for Georgiana.

Lizzy could only suppose that Lady Catherine wanted to prevent Caroline dominating Darcy's attention for the entire outing.

"Unexceptionable," agreed Caroline. "And we need not trouble Miss Bennet to go, since Miss Darcy's companion—such a genteel woman!—would make our fourth for the carriage."

The explanation of Mrs. Annesley's unfortunate accident and enforced rest burst on Caroline like a rain shower. Her teeth clamped shut with an audible click.

But Darcy eventually acquiesced and Caroline's teeth unlocked despite Lizzy's inclusion in the plan. The ladies took themselves off to change into appropriate race day wear.

Lizzy informed Mrs. Annesley of the day's new plan, and then, at the older lady's suggestion, went to offer her assistance to Miss de Bourgh. As a companion, Lizzy wasn't quite sure where the maid's services and her own overlapped. It was no part of Lizzy's duties to help Anne dress, for instance, but what about carrying her pelisse when it wasn't wanted or reminding her to put a fresh handkerchief in her reticule?

Anne's girl was just finished wrapping her in two shawls, and Anne herself put smelling salts, handkerchief, and fan in a beautiful, gold-filigreed reticule. Her face didn't look precisely happy, but it showed rather more animation than normal, and certainly her movements were brisker.

"Do you enjoy going to races?" Lizzy asked curiously.

Anne adjusted her bonnet, and the maid used several long pins to secure it, in addition to the bow beneath Anne's somewhat receding chin. "I have only been twice," Anne said. "But yes, I believe I do. I picked the winner four times when I went with my uncle."

"How exciting! You must tell me how you do it. I have sometimes wagered on the races in Hertfordshire, just with my sisters, and I must confess to being no judge of a horse."

Anne did not snub her, as Lizzy more than half expected. "I do enjoy horses," Anne admitted stiffly. "Our groom has always chosen my horses, most carefully bred for a lady, and driving them is one of my chief pleasures."

Anne looked almost pretty as she said this, almost happy.

"I am so glad Mr. Bingley should have suggested it, then."

Lizzy and Anne entered the parlor in advance of the others, and Lady Catherine looked Lizzy over critically, barely sparing an approving nod to her daughter.

"Miss Bennet," she commanded, "in the absence of Mrs. Annesley, I must make it clear that you should not leave my daughter or my niece at any time. Miss Darcy is not yet out, and although I allow this excursion, I should be most displeased if she should... well, I will not have that man sitting in her pocket! For a Darcy of Pemberley to make an alliance with a Bingley... who are they, pray? Who are their parents and grandparents? No. Georgiana is destined for a greater match than that."

That Lady Catherine might feel some awkwardness at having this conversation with Lizzy was only natural, but Lady Catherine appeared sublimely unaware, or perhaps uncaring, of such things. And it was obvious to Lizzy that the corollary of this little speech was that Caroline would never do for Darcy.

In Caroline, Lady Catherine recognized a serious danger—a woman of refinement, fortune, and style. In her mind, no doubt, Caroline was far more of a threat than Lizzy could ever have been.

"You are no fool, Miss Bennet," she continued, "so I don't hesitate to be forthright. Anne, I do not worry about you, you are much too mindful of your breeding and duty to allow such encroaching. But Georgiana is young, and I fear much given to sentiment."

Lady Catherine was cut off by the entrance of the rest of the party and Lizzy could only be glad. Poor Miss Darcy would be rendered acutely uncomfortable if she realized she was the topic of *that* discussion!

Whether Georgiana had any partiality for Mr. Bingley, Lizzy doubted. Mr. Bingley had spent the prior fall enthralled with Jane, and Miss Darcy had, not so long ago, fancied herself in love with Wickham. There would hardly have been time. The only one who wanted a match there was Caroline.

Mr. Darcy was not above enjoying a good race, though he was no gambler. He paid the entrance fee for the carriage when he arrived. The men on horseback and those on foot were not charged. The fee bought them a carriage space with a good view of the racecourse, but he also paid the small fee for a place in the covered grandstand, where the ladies could sit away from the common crowd and be protected in case of rain.

Thither they escorted the ladies and up to the bench his ticket indicated. Bingley enlivened the party with a description of the several horses he was disposed to favor, their last races, and their current chances. Bingley was not a serious gambler either, partly due to Darcy's judicious discouragement over the last few years, but he loved a good race and enjoyed the sport for its own sake. He was livelier than he'd been for many a week, and Darcy suspected it wasn't all to do with the races, but rather with the sudden renewal of his hopes regarding Miss Jane Bennet.

Darcy hadn't been to the Ashford racecourse before. He found it to be much quieter than Newmarket or Egham, and indeed, perfectly innocuous for Georgiana. The bulk of the attendees milled about on the ground, and the grandstand was less than half-filled with country squires and other genteel but unpretentious Kentish folk.

On the high ground at the south end of the racecourse were several rows of quality carriages, but no arms were blazed on the doors. Only a few looked as if they might have been driven down from London.

The races were already begun, of course, and the ladies were soon engrossed. That is, Georgiana and Anne and Elizabeth, who sat on the farthest end of the bench from himself, seemed to be engrossed. Caroline professed to be all excitement but continually called his attention to this spectator or that carriage at crucial moments.

"I say, look at that woman's hat," she said quietly, leaning close to make herself heard. "It must have eight ostrich feathers and her dress so orange as to eclipse the sun!"

Mr. Darcy turned his attention back to the race without reply. Most of her comments were in the same supercilious, mocking vein. Had she always been above her company? He did not remember her that way, but perhaps he only noticed now that... now that Elizabeth had so thoroughly humbled him.

A quick glance at Elizabeth distracted him more thoroughly than Caroline had ever done. Elizabeth was on the edge of the bench nearest to the far aisle, as was proper for a companion who cared about protecting her charges. This position, however, left her open to those who were coming and going on that stair. Even as he watched, two fashionable gentlemen paused and began speaking with her.

He could not hear what they said. Although Elizabeth was not encouraging them, barely replying and largely keeping her eyes on the race, he could not help a stab of anger. The two men clearly admired her and even her short replies, accompanied by her enchanting, flushed face, still warm from the exertion of climbing, were obviously enough to keep them there. What bad manners to speak to a woman they'd never been introduced to! They would not do it if they thought her of rank. Whether it was her somewhat plain dress, bonnet, or position on the bench, they apparently thought her open to insult.

Darcy tapped Colonel Fitzwilliam on the shoulder to take his place and excused himself. He went up a few steps to cross over and came down the stairs next to Elizabeth. It was unacceptable to leave a lady of their party so exposed. He should have realized when they sat down.

The crowd, which before struck him as provincial and unexciting, seemed suddenly full of overconfident young bucks.

"Excuse me," Darcy said, with an emphasis that caused both young men to excuse themselves. "Cousin Anne, Georgiana, would you please move down a trifle?"

They all moved, and Darcy sat down next to Elizabeth. It would be foolish to say he wasn't better pleased with this position, but he felt fully justified, knowing that he would have done the same for any woman under his temporary protection. If it had been Mrs. Annesley on the end, for instance, he would have done the same. It would not have been *necessary* with Mrs. Annesley, however, for she looked a proper companion and would not have attracted any notice.

Elizabeth was far too young and beautiful for this position.

"Thank you." Elizabeth shifted a little, eyes resolutely on the racecourse though the previous race had finished and now was only the controlled chaos of setting up for the next. "I did not encourage them."

"I know," Darcy replied quietly.

{ 18 }

To say Lizzy enjoyed the Ashford races would not be entirely accurate. To be sure, a bit of excitement, fresh air, and activity was a welcome interruption to their somewhat tedious routine in Tunbridge. Furthermore, Lizzy was genuinely pleased to see Anne enjoy herself. A day at the races, where she could sit without undo exertion and predict the outcome of the races (with the attendant compliments on her perspicacity), was just to Anne's liking.

Georgiana, situated between Bingley and Anne and later between Bingley and Caroline, also had a pleasant day. She was a little shy of Mr. Bingley. She did not know him well; she thought of him as "a friend of her brother" and was not yet accustomed to thinking of such people as possible friends of herself. The one notable and catastrophic exception to this mindset had been Mr. Wickham. But Mr. Bingley was jovial and friendly, without being in any way particular, and she passed a pleasant afternoon with him.

Lizzy's emotions were a little too complicated for her enjoyment. Mr. Darcy was not back to his pre-proposal talkativeness, but he was not entirely silent. He seemed to be making more of an effort than he had since the abbey, and she tried to respond suitably as they spent the better part of two hours making tentative conversation.

It was Caroline who was most to be pitied. She looked downright cross by the time they decided to stretch their legs and take a turn around the grounds. Mr. Darcy had noted a comfortable hotel in the nearby village and suggested the ladies might enjoy a little refreshment and rest there.

Anne, despite, or perhaps because of her unusual liveliness, was quite tired, and Mr. Darcy procured her a room where she might lie down for half an hour. For the rest, he hired a private parlor where they could have an early tea before they returned to the races.

Caroline did the honors of the tea service, but Mr. Bingley showed a tendency to gravitate towards Lizzy. He wanted to speak of Jane, she believed, but settled for Hertfordshire.

"I've half-decided to spend most of the season at Netherfield rather than London this year." He ate a bite of the delicious scones the hotel had provided. "Will your family be fixed there this summer?"

Lizzy smiled. "My aunt and uncle are taking a trip the Lake District and have invited me to accompany them, but my sisters and my parents will be at home. Jane is excellent with our nieces and nephews and will take charge of them while we are away."

"I'm sure she must be," he exclaimed. "So patient and happy as she is. That is to say, I'm sure they will enjoy time with all your sisters."

Caroline interjected, "This is the aunt and uncle from London? The barrister?"

"Yes," Lizzy answered with a level look. "They are quite my favorite family. Did my aunt look well when you called at their house? Jane tells me she was subject to a lingering cold this winter."

Caroline refilled her teacup gracefully, though her cheek paled a little. "She seemed quite well."

An awkward pause was filled unexpectedly by Georgiana. "I'm sure I wouldn't trade my brother for anything, but I quite envy you your sisters, Miss Elizabeth. How— how wonderful to have such sisterly affection and—and friendship."

Caroline pounced upon this heroic little speech. "I cannot say enough about sisterly affection. My dear Louisa and I have been the closest of friends since childhood. Indeed, nothing can equal our felicity, unless it be when dear Charles shall marry and give us another sister." She laid an affectionate hand on Miss Darcy's knee as she said this, but in that, Lizzy observed, she overplayed her hand.

Georgiana looked at Bingley with startled apprehension. Bingley's brow furrowed. Darcy always controlled his expression, but Lizzy thought there was a sudden look of comprehension in his deep brown eyes.

He brought his cup to Caroline to be refilled. "You must hope he will do so," he said prosaically. "But I admit I am not eager for a brother. I must beg Georgiana not to think of presenting me with one for at least another ten years or so."

"Ten years?" Caroline echoed playfully. "But she will be quite on the shelf."

"I am afraid my elasticity of mind is waning as I get older. It will take me at least that long to accustom myself to the idea of giving her away."

"But you must accustom yourself to that. Georgiana is to be presented next year, is she not? You won't make her spend another summer in Ramsgate."

Miss Darcy had turned a dull red.

"It is not decided," Mr. Darcy said.

Colonel Fitzwilliam came in swinging. "The thing is that my mother, Lady Fitzwilliam, and our Aunt Branford cannot decide who should have the honor of presenting Miss Darcy. I only ask that you take your time to decide, Georgiana, four or five seasons at least, as otherwise they will turn their attention upon me." He gave a theatrical grimace. "I do not relish the thought of their matrimonial focus trained in my direction."

This sally made them all smile but did not deter Miss Bingley. "It would solve all, Mr. Darcy, were you to take a wife. Then she would be the proper person to introduce my dear Miss Darcy."

Mr. Darcy cast his eyes up. "If Georgiana were to wait for that, she would wait a long time."

This silenced Caroline for the moment.

Lizzy felt a genuine spurt of sympathy for Mr. Darcy, along with a tiny bit of pride that he had asked to court *her*. If Lizzy had so chosen, *she* might have been the one to introduce Georgiana, a thought so foreign it almost made her laugh. It had not previously occurred to her that in proposing, he was inviting Lizzy to be part of his family, to be Georgiana's sister, and to be his partner in taking care of her.

Also, based on his look of impatient contempt, she gathered that Caroline was not the first to make such blatant hints in his direction. Perhaps he had been blinded to Caroline's previous hints because of his close friendship with Mr. Bingley, but clearly his eyes were opened now. And really, if many women treated him this way, and Lizzy did not doubt they did, was it any wonder he'd expected her to accept him at once?

Corrie Garrett

Thankfully Anne came down soon after and they returned to the races and, not long after that, to the carriage and back to Tunbridge.

{ 160 }

{ 19 }

DARCY WAS NOT TOTALLY surprised when Georgiana asked to speak to him alone. She fiddled with her shawl, folding it this way and that.

"Miss Bingley does not... does not know about Ramsgate, does she?"

"No, definitely not. You know neither the Colonel nor I would say anything."

"No, it is only—" She trailed off before starting again, stronger. "I do not excel at speaking plainly, but I desire to improve, so I must practice. Miss Bingley implied that her brother might offer for *me*. Is she correct? Do you have any reason to think so? Please do not conceal it from me if you do."

Poor girl. Mr. Darcy wrapped an arm around her shoulders. "Definitely not. Charles is a capital fellow, but I wouldn't make such a plan for you so soon after... well, everything. I was joking about ten years, but I am in no rush to see you wed. Indeed, you need never wed, if you do not like it. We have not spoken much of this, but you know that you are always welcome at Pemberley, and that you are an heiress in your own right. You will have more freedom in your future than many young women."

Her brows rose at the word "freedom." It must seem very strange to her after years of governesses and then the strict young ladies' seminary she had attended. The only real freedom she'd had was in Ramsgate, and that had gone poorly.

"Mr. Bingley has no expectation of offering for me?"

"None at all, I assure you. In fact," Mr. Darcy smiled grimly, "and I know you will not share this with anyone, but I should not be surprised if he eventually offers for Miss Jane Bennet, Miss Elizabeth's older sister."

Her mouth puckered with wonder. "Caroline will dislike it excessively."

He laughed. "That is plain-speaking, indeed! When did you get so astute? Or did Caroline tell you so?"

"No, no. She always described Jane Bennet as a sweet, simple girl, but she said *such* things of her mother and family! Caroline always spoke as if she pitied Miss Bennet and rather *enjoyed* the pity, if that makes sense."

"It does." Darcy eyed his sister, thinking she seemed more on the cusp of adulthood now than she had when she'd thought herself "grown-up" enough to elope. "When did you become so enamored of plain-speaking, Georgiana?"

"I suppose... I suppose it was Miss Elizabeth. She is a most extraordinary young lady, isn't she? I did try to dislike her, for your sake," Georgiana looked down, embarrassed, "but I could not."

Darcy tried to turn it off lightly, though her words struck him deeply. "No need for that. I still consider her one of the finest ladies of my acquaintance and there is no reason you ought not approve her. And I like to hear you speak so forthrightly. You remind me of our mother, you know."

Georgiana embraced him impulsively before they went down to a late dinner.

Lizzy did not *at all* mean to eavesdrop that evening when she left the parlor to retrieve Anne's better pillow and Georgiana's sketchbook.

Georgiana had expressed a wish to sketch the exquisite bouquet of High Weald wildflowers which a country urchin had presented to her when they were leaving the races.

Caroline had turned up her nose at such plebeian flowers and expressed a preference for the hothouse lilies which were grown at Pemberley.

"Yes, of course those are beautiful," Georgiana agreed. "But there is something so unstudied with these. Bluebells and primrose and yellow archangels..."

"May I fetch your sketch book, Miss Darcy?" Lizzy had offered. "I am just running upstairs for Anne's cushion."

She'd seen a moment of hesitation and expected to be quietly rebuffed. Instead, Georgiana raised her chin and smiled uncertainly. "Why, yes, if it's no trouble."

Caroline leaned forward. "Of course it's no trouble! That is what she's paid for, after all. Miss Bennet will be thinking you a loony, my dear."

Miss Darcy covered her confusion with a cough, but Lizzy was becoming inured to such remarks. "Only a loony for thinking I shouldn't be happy to do a favor for a friend," Lizzy added, over her shoulder.

As she left the room, she heard Caroline continue, "I declare I must show you one of my own little sketches. You must tell me what you think of my *chiaroscuro*."

Lizzy found the cushion for Anne by the fire in her room and then went to Miss Darcy's room. The sketch book was a little harder to find, but Lizzy found it eventually, where a maid had pushed it into an unlikely drawer in the desk. Lizzy went across to Mrs. Annesley's room, just for a moment, to let that good lady know that her charge was in excellent spirits.

At the bottom of the stairs, just past the sharp right turn that led to the row of private parlors, Lizzy heard her name. She looked back toward the stairs, thinking someone had called her.

Caroline and Darcy were coming down. "Miss Bennet?" Caroline repeated carelessly. "Pray what did I say amiss?"

Mr. Darcy replied in a lower tone than hers and Lizzy could not quite make it out, but she heard Caroline's reply. "Why should that distress dear Georgiana? Darcy, you are not making sense, unless your admiration for Miss Eliza and her fine eyes has rekindled, in which case I can only wish you happiness. Your mother-in-law will be ecstatic. When does she arrive?"

The words were dripping with sarcasm and Lizzy hurried on, not wanting to hear more.

She'd heard quite enough. Mr. Darcy was chastising Caroline for belittling her. What a comedown for the haughty Miss Bingley! And even stranger was the tone of her teasing about his admiration. It had the tenor of a long-standing joke, and Lizzy wasn't sure whether she was more mortified that they had mocked her mother, or more flattered that he'd made his admiration for Lizzy's eyes known to Miss Bingley months ago.

Mr. Darcy decided to sit next to Elizabeth when he entered the parlor again. It was rather to punish Miss Bingley than from any other motive. That lady needed a salutary set-down. He could not easily converse with Elizabeth anymore, if indeed they had ever had anything of ease, but he sat next to her observing those who were speaking for some silent minutes.

"The question is, sir," Elizabeth said, as if they were in the middle of the conversation, "whether you punish Miss Bingley or yourself more in sitting here."

His brows rose. Punish himself? Did she refer to the regret and disappointment he still felt in her presence? The awkwardness of knowing that she, of all women the one he preferred, had seen his flaws most clearly?

"I mean," she continued, "that there are Mr. Bingley and Colonel Fitzwilliam discussing enclosure, on which I assume you must have decided opinions, and yet you are situated a bit too far to join in their discussion."

Mr. Darcy shifted toward her. "I was not aware of what they were speaking."

"And yet your eyes have been on them these ten minutes at least. What occupies your thoughts, then?"

She occupied his thoughts. When he sat by her thus, he was acutely aware of every inch of bench between them, of her movements and expressions, of the lavender scent of her clothes.

Mr. Darcy smiled slightly. "I was simply absent-minded, I'm afraid."

His plan for leaving Tunbridge with inner serenity and indifference seemed farther afield than ever.

{ 20 }

*D*EAR *CHARLOTTE*,

    I apologize for being a dilatory correspondent! You will not believe (or perhaps you will) who has come to stay in Tunbridge, at our very hotel; it is Charles and Caroline Bingley. I know I told you of her rather transparent interest in Mr. Darcy which I observed at Netherfield; her behavior here is all of a piece. If he could be got by smiles and compliments and innuendoes, not to mention slavish attention to his sister, he would be got.

    On a more serious topic, I must admit that my slowness in responding to your last letter is not mere thoughtlessness but pride. I feel that you may indeed have been correct about Jane and Mr. Bingley, and that if he had been more certain of her feelings, it would have been for the best. However, I am tolerably hopeful that he may visit Jane when he returns to London.

What other news have I? Not much, I fear. Mr. Darcy took us to the races, and I discovered that Miss de Bourgh could build a second fortune as a gambler if she so chose.

Lizzy bit her lip. There was so much she could not discuss with Charlotte. Unthinkable to share that Lizzy had rejected Mr. Darcy. Charlotte, who had settled for Mr. Collins, would condemn the decision whole-heartedly. Lizzie did not feel sanguine enough to make light of it yet, nor did Lizzy want to ridicule Mr. Darcy's proposal. Mr. Darcy ought not to be made sport of in that way, especially when Lizzy herself had been so at fault.

She also could not bring herself to talk about Mr. Darcy's influence, now being used for good, which might help reunite Jane and Mr. Bingley.

With Charlotte's marriage to Mr. Collins, their correspondence had grown increasingly light. Lizzy no longer felt she could share the depths of herself with her old friend. She missed having a confidante. She missed having a friend.

Lizzy finished her letter with commonplaces about the trip and questions as to Charlotte's health and happiness. Then it was on to another and even more unpleasant letter to her father.

After a few anecdotes which she knew her father would enjoy, Lizzy came to the point.

Jane wrote me of Lydia's plans to go to Brighton with Colonel Forster and his wife. Can you think this wise? She is silly amongst a single militia in her own village; will she not be vulgar and ridiculous, in the worst way, amongst a whole troop?

I know she would be livid were she to see this, but I feel I must ask you to reconsider your permission. You encouraged me to enlarge my acquaintance by traveling with the de Bourgh family; I have done so. I know you are concerned about the loss of our portions, and perhaps you think a larger acquaintance will offset this setback. Perhaps you are right. But I must say that Lydia's behavior, and Kitty as well, becomes ever more unacceptable, even more so if they have nothing. How will they ever be respected if they continue as they are now? Age will surely bring some level of maturity, I would hope, but we both know that age does not equal wisdom. I know that there would be a great fuss and outcry if you deny her, but if you, my dear father, will not check her now, I am very much afraid Lydia will be neither happy nor respectable in the future.

I can imagine you shaking your head over this, but please consider shaking your head at Lydia. She needs it far more than I do.

Much love,
Your Lizzy

Another morning in the pump room, another hour with Georgiana and Anne, the latter of whom now dutifully drank five tumblers of the water every morning before they returned to the hotel.

This morning, however, Georgiana gamely responded to Lizzy's attempts at conversation. She even described her life at the seminary and admitted that while she was an indifferent reader, she had excelled in the natural sciences.

"My brother says it is quite a modern school," Georgiana confided shyly. "They were very influenced by Rousseau and were continually telling us of the excellencies of the natural world. We were encouraged to walk every day and to spend great amounts of time outdoors."

Anne made a face, though whether it was at this description or the water was uncertain. "What a strange idea! My mama has no opinion of these new seminaries. She says decorum is no longer taught to the younger generation."

"We had lessons in deportment, music, dancing, and art. All the usual accomplishments," Miss Darcy said mildly.

From there they went on to music, to flowers, to botany, to gardening. For once, the morning time passed quickly.

The painter was there again.

"What an age portraits take!" Lizzy exclaimed. "This is the third time I've seen them. I feel quite sorry for that little boy."

Miss Darcy had been surreptitiously eyeing the painting. She brought her attention back to them with a start. "Hm?"

"Have you had your portrait taken, Miss Darcy?" Elizabeth asked.

"No... That is, yes, when our family's portrait was done about ten years ago. The artist stayed at Pemberley for a month, I believe, and we did four sittings. They must allow time between for the paint and glazing to dry. I daresay this is their final sitting."

"My mother's portrait was done by Sir Thomas Lawrence," Anne told them proudly.

Lady Catherine was just returning to them with her friend, and overheard this. "Indeed, it was. Now Sir Thomas is off painting generals and such on the continent. It would have been as well for him if he had stayed; I should have strongly counseled him to stay. I must have Anne's portrait taken soon."

"Oh, yes," her friend Mrs. Winkleigh agreed. "I have commissioned Mr. Turner to do a miniature of my son." She gestured to the painter. "Mr. Turner is quite the portraitist; his work was displayed at Somerset, you know. Mr. Winkleigh has a miniature of himself while he was at Oxford and wants a matching one of Reginald."

"My husband took me to the very first display at Somerset House," Lady Catherine said. "He was a friend of Sir William."

"I shall introduce you to Mr. Turner," Mrs. Winkleigh said.

Corrie Garrett

She performed the introduction while Mr. Turner's subjects took a break for refreshment.

Mr. Turner was a youngish man, not very tall or handsome, but with an intelligent, good-humored look to his eyes and forehead. He showed his smudged hands and apologized for being unable to properly greet them. He joked with Mrs. Winkleigh about painting her son on a stallion someday and was "deeply honored" at the prospect of painting for Lady Catherine, "honored to be considered, that is, whether she chose him or not."

As they were leaving, he asked Miss Darcy whether she was satisfied with the expression and shadows of the child's face.

"Oh, yes," Miss Darcy said, "I've attempted my cousin's children and never captured so much character. Not that I mean to compare— You are a professional."

He smiled quizzically. "You look rather familiar to me, Miss Darcy. I've never painted you before; I think I would remember that, but perhaps we've met?"

Georgiana blushed. "You are, perhaps, thinking of Miss Climping's School for Girls in Bath. I believe we met in passing there."

"Of course!" he said. "The arts mistress is my aunt. She had me judge some of the schoolgirls' pieces or some such thing before the summer term. I believe you won."

"You must have an uncommonly good memory," Miss Darcy said. "Only a week's work for you."

He laughed. "I'm afraid I don't remember your artwork, except that it was clearly superior to the rest and made my decision quite easy."

His patron returned and he bowed to them. "Good day, Miss Darcy. Miss Bennet."

Lizzy and Georgiana hurried to catch up with the rest of the party. Georgiana was still a little flushed.

"Did you recognize Mr. Turner from the outset?" Lizzy asked. "When we saw him last week?"

"Y-yes. I did not expect he would remember me or—or even the occasion."

She put up a hand to keep her hat from slipping.

"That is a charming hat." Lizzy took pity on Georgiana and changed the subject. "I've been admiring it all morning."

"Oh, thank you! Your bonnet is charming as well." She muttered something else, but so softly that Lizzy only caught a few words about her "brother noticing."

Lizzy flushed lightly. "Do you know how much longer you will be with us in Tunbridge, Miss Darcy?"

"I am not certain. My brother had said something of returning to London this week and thence to Pemberley, but he did not expect Mr. and Miss Bingley. He says it would be rude to leave on the instant."

"That is considerate of him. And I am selfishly glad to have you for a few more days."

"He – he *is* considerate, you know." Georgiana took a deep breath and straightened her hat with trembling fingers. "I made up my mind that I ought, before we go, to explain something to you—"

"Miss Darcy, you have no obligation, no need to distress yourself."

"No, but…if someone you care about is unhappy…we have a duty to do what we must, no? And this is not about him, but me." Georgiana explained a little of what had passed, her foolish infatuation with Wickham, though she did not use his name, and Darcy's kindness in dealing with it. "I say this only to explain—to show—that he is the kindest, most loyal brother a girl could have."

Lizzy would have stopped her more quickly, but she felt that this confession was a brave step for Miss Darcy. The younger girl might be the better for having unburdened herself a trifle. Oh, the times Lizzy and Jane had stayed up until the wee hours sharing their thoughts and dreams and sorrows! There was really nothing like a sister. Lizzy again felt the slight pang of loss that she might have truly been Georgiana's sister, if she'd accepted Mr. Darcy.

When Georgiana stopped, Lizzy took her hand, squeezing it fondly. "I must admit that I shouldn't imagine anyone who knew you would blame you for such a tangle! What a frightful situation. How thankful I am that you escaped."

"Thank you! But I only tell you this so that you see, when my brother cares about someone, nothing else matters. Even when they have erred..." Miss Darcy was almost inaudible now.

Lizzy walked arm and arm with her and bumped her playfully. "An effective homily, Mr. Parson, with an excellent illustration. You are a very good sister." Privately, Lizzy felt a little sorry for Miss Darcy's naivete. She would learn all too soon that even in matters of love, no one could truthfully say "nothing else matters." Circumstances *did* matter. Family, fortune, faith, and folly... there were a thousand things that mattered more than affection.

Good heavens, Lizzy sounded like Charlotte.

They were almost back to the hotel, and Miss Darcy had clearly reached the end of her courage, which had been quite impressive.

"My dear Miss Darcy—goodness, I sound like Miss Bingley when I say that!—I can't tell you how much your trust means to me. I hope that we can be good friends whatever may happen in the future. I think that you are quite the sweetest, most loyal sister a brother could ever have."

"Oh, no. He is so good, so patient, Miss Bennet."

"But you must call me Elizabeth, I insist, for we are indeed friends now. Or rather Lizzy, if you choose. And may I call you Georgiana?"

"Yes, please."

{ 21 }

I F THE NEW EASE BETWEEN HIS sister and Miss Elizabeth could be believed, they had somehow become fast friends. It was what Darcy had always hoped Caroline might become for Georgiana but had never materialized. Caroline had certainly tried to befriend Georgiana, but Darcy did not blame Georgiana for never warming up to her. What Caroline had not achieved in the several years of their acquaintance, Elizabeth had achieved in a matter of weeks.

Tonight, however, Georgiana had been obliged to stay behind, as she was not yet out. Lady Catherine had decided to take Anne (and the rest of their party) to the opening assembly of the Tunbridge Wells' season.

Darcy thought calling it a "season" was rather too grand now that Tunbridge was so out of fashion. In Darcy's grandfather's time, Beau Nash had made Tunbridge quite a hub of the peerage, but those days were long over. This was merely the start of the assemblies and small public balls that would enliven the quiet watering hole, and Lady Catherine wanted to be seen there.

Darcy didn't love public assemblies, but he had several London acquaintances here, as well as Chuff and Honoria, so he passed a tolerable hour before the dancing was to begin.

Anne did not intend to dance, of course; her delicate health precluded it. Darcy stood up first with his cousin Honoria.

"I can grant you the two first, Darcy," she said roguishly, "because no one stands up with their husband first. But then I really must return to my dear Chuff, and you must brave the wide ocean."

"Do you call yourself a fish, cousin?"

"On the contrary, *you* are the fish, and you must choose who you will be caught by when I throw you back."

He didn't so much as flick his eyes in Elizabeth's direction, but she did, nodding to where Elizabeth sat against the wall beside Anne. "I like that girl. You could do much worse. Like that odiously consequential Miss Bingley."

Darcy bit back a groan. "I might accept this kind of interference from my aunt, but you are just my meddlesome cousin. I do not have to put up with it."

"Oh, Fitz."

"If you tread into nicknames, I can follow you, *Horrie.*"

"Oh! That does take me back to childhood."

"Perhaps it will take you back to a recollection that I am my own man and do not need all these suggestions."

"*All these suggestions*? But I have only this instant said anything! It is too unfair of you. You mustn't blame me for the interference of others."

Darcy just eyed her silently, knowing how much she enjoyed teasing him.

She continued with a twinkle. "Now, if perchance more than one of your friends have hinted in the same direction, that is only serendipity."

He maintained his silence, twirling her through the set.

"Oh, come now, I am *so* curious," she said. "I've been out of the world with the twins, you know, so you must allow me a little fun."

"I do, but…" Darcy suddenly felt weary. Perhaps if he had not yet declared himself to Elizabeth and was still in that state of confident ignorance, he might have found her playful banter less… exhausting. "She declined, Horrie. So have your fun, but please do not have it at my expense."

His graceful cousin missed a step in the dance and had to scurry to catch up. She gave him a speaking look, half-sympathy and half-exasperation, but the end of the dance was coming up and there was not much more time for conversation.

When he returned her to Chuff, she looked downright thoughtful. Darcy kissed her cheek. "Don't worry. Enjoy your next dance."

She smiled a little and Darcy moved off. It was incumbent on him to ask for Caroline's hand at some point, but she was already engaged with another gentleman for this set, so he returned to stand by Lady Catherine and watch.

Bingley was dancing with the prettiest girl in the room, as he often seemed to do. He was gay and lively, already bidding fair to become a Tunbridge favorite, but there was something different in his manner than formerly. He was clearly in the best of good spirits, but he did not look at his partners the way he had looked at Jane. He smiled, moved on, and smiled again. There was no particularity, no intent gaze, no quiet compliment to make a female heart flutter.

His friend was not dancing like a bachelor anymore. He danced like a man whose decision was made. Bingley also stood up once with Elizabeth, and Darcy tried to be disinterestedly glad that she had the chance to dance.

At the end of the current set, Caroline's partner brought her back and Darcy promptly asked for the next, rather in the manner of a man downing his medicine in one go.

Caroline simpered and fanned herself. Over her shoulder, Darcy saw Chuff extend a hand to Elizabeth.

Darcy narrowed his eyes. Was Honoria behind that? What mortifying mischief was she brewing? Elizabeth didn't seem to demur very much, and as Lady Catherine didn't object, she soon stood up with his friend.

Maybe Darcy was being overly sensitive. Chuff had met Elizabeth on several occasions now and was free to ask her to dance if he liked.

Darcy moved somewhat mechanically through the dance with Caroline. She was telling him one of the rumors currently in circulation in London drawing rooms.

"I daresay it's not true, but I for one believe it. She turned him down *four* times before accepting his offer, and everyone knew he was mad for her. No wonder he should be so jealous as to sell her carriage..." she continued, but Darcy didn't attend. It was just slanderous gossip, neither interesting nor, likely, accurate.

At the end of their dance, Chuff guided Elizabeth to them on the dance floor and bowed to Miss Bingley. "I say, Darcy, will you introduce your partner to me? I've not had the honor."

After the introduction, Chuff solicited Miss Bingley for the next dance, leaving Elizabeth and him quite alone in the middle of the dance floor.

"Excuse me," Lizzy said. "I should return to Lady Catherine—"

"Will you dance with me, Miss Bennet, if I remember to comment on the number of couples or perhaps the weather?"

She laughed uncertainly. "You have an uncanny memory for my remarks."

He held out his hand and was shaken with both pleasure and pain when she slid hers into his.

Darcy did not actually comment on the size of the room or the number of couples. He did thank her for her kindness to Georgiana. "She is not confident—not that I should wish her to be that arrogant sort of debutante one sees, who finds the whole world a bore—but she is often shy to the point of isolation. I am glad to see her making a friend."

"It's a pleasure. She is shy and uncertain, as you say, but I think she has the potential to be a… young woman of sound understanding."

"That would please me immensely."

Elizabeth intuitively understood that what he wanted for Georgiana most was not beauty or poise or conquests. He wanted her to be discerning. He wanted her to be a woman that earned respect as well as affection.

Elizabeth nodded. "She is most loyal to you. I fancy the root of that is mainly in her own sweet nature," she smiled cheekily, "but some part of it must be due to you. It is quite the best thing I know of you."

Darcy shook his head. "I have done all I ought for her, but I know it is not what our mother would have done."

"No, you could not fill that role, but clearly she loves you and feels loved by you; that is far more than 'doing all you ought,' and far more than many young ladies receive."

The rest of the assembly room was becoming a blur, as if he had had too much to drink or too little.

"I do not think," Darcy said, "that I can calmly discuss love with you. Even brotherly love."

She flushed. "I apologize. I hope that, despite the unfortunate nature of our early acquaintance, we can be friends—"

"Elizabeth," Darcy cut in. "I beg your pardon, but you don't owe me an apology. If you—If your opinion of me has changed at all, if you find that you could perhaps accept what I once offered, please tell me. I have never had any but contempt for men who persecute women with their attention, but I would rue it forever if my pride kept me from asking once more. If my pride kept me from the possibility of your acceptance."

The dance separated them for a moment, and her face was white when they returned.

"Blast. I should not be doing this during a dance," Darcy muttered for her only. "Thus I humiliate myself twice. But if you feel that you could accept me, I would be the happiest of men. I know my behavior, my manners, have not been what they ought. But if you can forgive me... please believe that my admiration and love have been and remain wholly yours."

{ 22 }

LIZZY'S FEET AUTOMATICALLY performed the end of the dance which came at those words. The applause of the crowd and the heat of the bodies surrounded her. Lizzy's every sense was heightened.

She caught the genuine laugh Caroline was giving Chuff. She smelled the smoke of the many gas lamps. She saw Lady Honoria walk by with a sideways glance. Lady Catherine and Anne were statues in the distance. Lizzy's own hands raised automatically to clap with the others. Her palms were cold and damp, but she still felt the ghostly warmth of Mr. Darcy's hands on hers. She saw the wavering uncertainty of his look, half agony, half hope. Completely gone was the arrogant man she'd once thought him to be. Here was the living, breathing, flawed but fascinating man she'd come to know.

He would not ask again; she was sure of it. He was not the sort to repeatedly throw his heart on the ground, and she was not the sort of "elegant female" who rejected for the purpose of prolonging the game.

The problem was—did she love him? She wasn't sure. She was well on her way to falling for Georgiana, but that was not a reason to accept. She certainly felt respect and yes, something like affection and attraction. But was it love? But when she thought of rejecting him, of losing him forever, her heart recoiled.

As the applause died down, Lizzy said quietly, "My— my feelings have undergone such a transformation, that I can hardly express it. You must know that I realize how mistaken I was. If you do still desire to… to marry me, I would be honored."

Darcy gripped her hand, eyes blazing, and for a startled moment she thought he might kiss her right there in front of everyone.

It seemed amazing that the whole room didn't stop to listen and watch. How could everyone not realize what a cataclysmic thing had just happened?

Darcy did not kiss her, but he did tuck her hand in the crook of his arm and press her fingers, while leading her somewhat haphazardly off the dance floor. If either of them noted where they were going or who they passed, it was more than she would vouch for.

"You have made me very happy. I can hardly…" he trailed off as they passed another of his acquaintances. "I have never found an assembly more irksome!

Refreshments?" He led her in that direction. It was a perfectly innocuous task and gave them both a few moments for pounding hearts to calm and racing thoughts to ease.

"I am... beyond glad," he finally managed. "I will write to your father at once, if you have no objection. Or if you think it better, I could visit him when I take Georgiana north."

"Oh." Lizzy felt a bucket of cold-water slosh into her stomach. "A letter, I think. Yes, and I will write to him also." The thought of Darcy speaking to her father before he had been warned curdled the milk of imagination. Her father would simply not believe it. He might not even believe her letter, but at least if Darcy wrote, she would have time to corroborate.

Darcy handed her a glass of lemonade, and Lizzy sipped it slowly. "Your aunt," she said, "will be dissatisfied." A gross understatement.

Darcy's look was stern, though she was beginning to learn it did not denote disapproval. "If you were under another roof, her opinion would be a matter of indifference to us. As it is... perhaps we should wait to inform her until I have your father's blessing."

"When I shall hopefully be away from here."

"But of course," Darcy said blankly. "You must resign at once."

"At once? But, perhaps I ought not. It seems careless and ungrateful to leave all at once." Though on the other hand, she certainly didn't owe Lady Catherine any extraordinary degree of civility, considering how badly she had treated Lizzy. Oh, Lady Catherine would be beyond furious when she learned of this!

Lizzy pressed a cool hand to her overheated forehead. "I think I need time to consider. I am finding it difficult to believe that we are actually… that we…" Lizzy had never found herself so inarticulate.

Darcy smiled. "Is it possible that I have rendered Miss Elizabeth Bennet speechless?"

"I think you have. You ought to enjoy it, for I warn you that it is most unusual."

"I know, and I do. Have I told you yet that you are by far the most beautiful woman in the room?"

Lizzy felt her face heat even more. She would never have expected Mr. Darcy to be a tease.

He leaned close to say in her ear, "You have rendered me speechless on more than one occasion. This is only fair."

"Mr. Darcy, people will stare. I never thought I should be the one to preach decorum to you." Lizzy curtseyed to him. "I must have time to reflect. I shall return to Lady Catherine and Miss de Bourgh."

She moved away and managed not to look behind her or to bump into too many innocent bystanders. Lady Catherine was thankfully engaged in a conversation and so

Lizzy was able to slip back into her chair next to Anne without comment.

She tried to present a calm, complacent mien to the world. It was one of the hardest things she had ever done. Mr. Darcy! He had asked again! And she had accepted him!

Lizzy couldn't help pressing cool fingers to her cheeks once or twice, trying to force back some of the telling color she could feel staining her cheeks.

She had accepted Mr. Darcy. Her amazement was no less that he had asked again than that she had accepted. Certainly her views of him had changed, and her heart had given that violent twinge. Was this love?

Well, it was something very disturbing. It made her feel distinctly light-headed, wobbly, and warm. It also seemed to be affecting her vision, turning the assembly room into a colorful blur. Was not general decrepitude a sure sign of love?

Well, it was done. He'd been accepted, and she would not draw back. Her heated cheeks cooled and the dazzling swirl of color and light resolved into the usual swirl of dancing couples and lamps.

She found her emotions swung like the pendulum on the grandfather clock in her father's study. When she dwelt on the prospect of being Georgiana's sister, she felt immense satisfaction and even anticipation. She felt she might be a real friend to Georgiana and the younger girl to her. But then she questioned why *Georgiana,* who at best was only tangentially related to their marriage, was the focus of her first coherent thoughts? One did not get engaged because of an affection for a man's sister...!

Then she thought of being Mrs. Darcy; the stares and gossip she would endure in London and the prospect of becoming the mistress of his unknown but assuredly grand estate. She felt a trifle cold and breathless.

But when she thought of walking with him, talking with him, enjoying something more of the congeniality and warmth she now knew he possessed in addition to his intelligence... she felt giddy again. Lizzy believed they were capable through nature and intellect of a meeting of the minds, of true companionship. But what if he never unbent enough to enjoy that?

But surely... with as much as he had changed even in the last month, she should expect the best.

She did not try to catch his eye or attention for the rest of the assembly, but it was difficult to avoid. Both sets of eyes were drawn to the other as a pin to a magnet.

Mr. Darcy was more adept in the art of stoicism than she, but Lizzy spied that even he was more smiling, more genial, more bright and handsome than usual. To think she had made him so happy quite offset her misgivings and almost offset the looming upset of Lady Catherine's displeasure. Contemplating his obvious joy gave her nearly half an hour of uninterrupted tranquility, even when Mr. Darcy danced with other acquaintances. She could almost hear his thought process, that he had already been indiscreet enough to propose on a dance floor. The least he could do was to dance a few more times and mitigate the clear intentionality of his dance with her, at least until he had requested her hand from her father and could announce their engagement.

Her outward tranquility even remained when he came and stood near, conversing in a desultory fashion with his aunt and only allowing his eyes to stray her direction at discreet intervals. This was disrupted when Bingley and his sister came to join their group. Mr. Darcy, in the course of things, was forced to ask Caroline for a second dance.

Mr. Bingley held out his hand to Lizzy. "And will you dance again, Miss Elizabeth? I am tired of standing up with strangers."

"What, you, Mr. Bingley?" she asked "Has some strange magic switched the predilections of you and your friend? For Mr. Darcy has danced at least five dances and yet you are tired of strangers."

He smiled as they took their place in the set but spoke in a voice quieter than normal. "They none of them know the lady I am thinking of and are therefore useless to me, as my mind cannot be wrested away."

Elizabeth could not help a genuine laugh of delight at this bold speech. Oh, would she and Jane both find themselves with the joy of an unexpected engagement this year? Nothing could make her joy as complete as the thought of

Jane's happiness. "I can only be eager to be of such service, sir."

Bingley already looked embarrassed at his slightly brash statement. It was perhaps not the purest good manners to speak of a woman he was not certain of, a woman he had disappointed and not yet apologized to, but Lizzy, herself so happy, was ready to forgive.

"It is not a burden to me to talk of my sister, for I am missing her heartily. I do not think we have been apart this long in at least five years, when she spent a winter with my aunt and uncle."

"Not for the season?"

"No. My aunt and uncle don't rise to such circles. My aunt was unwell after the birth of her son, and Jane, even at seventeen, was able to be a great help to her. Unlike many ladies of sweet and yielding disposition, most children actually mind her."

"I cannot imagine how they could do otherwise!" Bingley declared.

Lizzy laughed. "I'm afraid that only shows how little you know of children. Most would trample a saint if she had not a loud voice. But Jane will begin a story, or a game, or a project with ribbons and acorns, and before they know where they are, they've passed an afternoon without vice."

They separated in the dance and Lizzy passed Mr. Darcy with a smile she could not conceal. He looked back at her, almost gratefully, as if he were already questioning whether she regretted her decision.

When the dance returned her to Mr. Bingley's side, he looked serious. She wondered if perhaps he had noted their interchange, but he seemed oblivious.

"I really must insist to Caroline that we return to London tomorrow. I cannot wait—That is, I need not conceal from you that I am all eagerness to—to visit with the elder Miss Bennet again."

Lizzy could not bring herself to commit to Jane's feelings on receiving him. Jane was ever humble and forgiving, but it was not Lizzy's place to say so.

"I hope that you will," she said instead. When the dance ended, Mr. Bingley walked her back to Lady Catherine. Mr. Darcy and Caroline also rejoined their small group.

Caroline smiled thinly at Lizzy. "I see that you are as fond of dancing as ever, Miss Elizabeth. A pity your sisters could not be here, but I daresay they would find it a trifle flat, young gentlemen being so scarce."

"That is every young lady's dread, is it not?" Lizzy answered. "You must be thankful to be at an age beyond such volatility."

"Quite."

Charles shrugged. "*I* am not beyond such volatility and would ask you to dance again, Miss Elizabeth, would it not set people to talking if we danced a third time."

Lizzy sketched a slight curtsey. "Then I give you credit for both the asking and the circumspection not to ask."

Caroline leaned on Darcy's arm. "I am sure so much dancing is a punishment to you, Mr. Darcy. Shall we sit out the last dances together, as we did in Hertfordshire?"

Lady Catherine stood. "While I myself am not overpowered by the heat of the room, I am sure it is not beneficial for Anne. We shall retire to the hotel."

{ 23 }

LIZZY LABORED OVER HER LETTER into the wee hours of the morning. At first, she tried to be fully serious, as indeed she felt, trying to explain the complete reversal in her opinion of Mr. Darcy. The letter did not feel right; it did not sound like herself. However she pictured her father reacting to it, she could not picture him responding well. Finally, Lizzy drew out a fresh sheet, her last, and allowed her natural humor, which rejoiced in the ridiculous even in her own life, to start on a lighter note.

Dear Papa,

You will have reason to gloat when you receive this letter, for I must confess that your request has been vindicated. Circumstances have conspired to make me supremely grateful for these last weeks spent with the de Bourgh family, which is a sentiment I never *thought to express. I know I wrote a silly but (fairly) dutiful letter upon the event of my sojourn to Tunbridge Wells, but I'm sure you realized my heart was not in it.*

Now, however, I am glad of it all and I must explain why.

I will start by saying that you must be happy for me. As I have established that I am giving you credit for the blessing that has befallen me, you must also bear whatever reproach may come with it.

The thing is that I have received an offer of marriage, contingent on your blessing, of course, and that his letter and mine may well reach you at the same time. If you do indeed have two letters upon your desk at this moment, you are no doubt looking at the other seal in blankest astonishment. If you have not, for some reason, received his letter, let me take the hurdle at once: the man is Mr. Darcy.

No, don't laugh, this is not a ridiculous jest I am playing out to amuse you, or even an elaborate joke to punish you.

It is true.

It comes about that Mr. Darcy is not at all the proud, disagreeable man we all thought him to be. I cannot excuse his behavior in Hertfordshire, but as I have now seen evidence of better qualities, I believe there were some mitigating circumstances. Namely, that he had just had a most distressing interlude with his sister, who was nearly ruined by a conniving family connection. He was in no very amiable humor to be meeting anyone. His behavior was still arrogant and rude, but he has apologized several times and I am now, being nearly a besotted fiancée, inclined to forgive him.

I can *still see his flaws, so perhaps I am not truly besotted, but I am indeed satisfied with my choice, and I pray you will be also. He is a far better man than I thought; in his behavior I have seen evidence of kindness, loyalty, honor, and even humility. If you had heard my animadversions on his character! That is, you did hear them in Hertfordshire, and I said most of them to him. And yet he never treated me with anything but respect, even when it must have smarted. He has humbled himself to admit that his pride has been at fault, and that his behavior was not at all what it should have been.*

More than that... well, I cannot exactly say what has put me in my current state, but I suspect you do not wish to hear me rhapsodize on his many qualities much longer.

I pray that you will quickly send us your response. I will thereafter travel to London, either by the Mail, or else possibly with Mr. Darcy and his sister, and from thence home to Hertfordshire. I have made no definite plans, but I know that Lady Catherine will be most unhappy with this development, and I would rather be away before the revelation is made. If I could possibly be absent from both her and my mother when the news is broken, so much the better, but I know I ought not expect miracles from this present fallen world.

Much love,
Lizzy

P.S. I do hope Mr. Darcy has expressed himself well. His heart, I believe, is in the right place, but the habit of years is not easily overcome. Please do not let it irk you if he should sound rather stiff. I believe that may be his chief flaw—a failure to unbend at the appropriate moment.

E. B.

In the course of the early morning, while Anne was putting on her hat to go to the bath house, and before Lady Catherine had come down, Lizzy slipped her letter to Mr. Darcy. He nodded gravely, but with a spark of something in his eye.

"I'll mail both today," he promised.

She smiled, somewhat uncertainly. In the clear light of morning, it seemed almost fantastical that last night had occurred. He was rich, handsome, and sought-after. Had he in fact begged her to marry him in the middle of a dance?

"Is something amiss?" he asked. There was a maid laying out breakfast things, and Colonel Fitzwilliam was lounging by the window with the London paper.

"No." Lizzy closed her eyes for a brief moment. "I was merely reflecting on what a strange thing sleep is. It makes all sorts of fanciful imaginings possible, but sometimes makes solid events seem like dreams."

Mr. Darcy's eyes warmed. "I have found that strange as well. And what do you think is the solution to that disquieting sensation?"

Lizzy chuckled. "Journaling?"

"How prosaic. I would prefer the corroboration of witnesses, at the very least."

Colonel Fitzwilliam cleared his throat as Lady Catherine entered, and Lizzy stepped away from Mr. Darcy. Did Colonel Fitzwilliam *know*? He must at least suspect, and Lizzy's cheeks warmed.

Lady Catherine eyed them but only recommended the Colonel to find his handkerchief if he would continue coughing.

Lizzy and Anne and Georgiana took their accustomed trek to the bath house, today accompanied by Lady Catherine and the gentlemen. Mr. Darcy's arm was bespoken by Lady Catherine for herself and Anne, and the Colonel offered his arms to Georgiana and Lizzy.

The pavement was washed clean from the rain the night before, and the already-charming fronts above the shops looked newly white-washed. A few puddles still lingered, rippled by a cool breeze that threaded its way down the Parade. Lizzy was thankful for her warm cloak this morning. She delighted in spring, with cool mornings and warm afternoons and soaking showers.

She wondered what the spring in Derbyshire would be like.

If Darcy were given to fanciful imaginings, he would have imagined that the letters in his breast pocket had an inexplicable weight and temperature. They seemed to be made of gold leaf and to have a pleasant warmth that was palpable through his vest and shirt.

He was a happy man this morning. To think that once he had looked on engagement to Elizabeth as a mixed blessing! Since it had been denied him once, he now felt the *full* blessing of having found such a treasure of a woman and all the good fortune of having her accept him.

The only fly in all this ointment was what to do with this damnable interval before her father's blessing was obtained and before she was restored to her family to begin preparations for a wedding.

He was not so eager to be thrust into the Bennet family circle, but he knew he must do it and with a good heart, to prove to Elizabeth that he truly was repentant for disparaging them so harshly. If it must be done, let it be done soon.

Once he had deposited the ladies at the bath house, he excused himself on a matter of business, and took himself off to post the letters.

He passed Chuff and Honoria with a bow, but he didn't stay to chat.

Darcy, who abhorred subterfuge and artifice, was not best pleased to have to dissemble with his friends. It was hopefully a matter of days until he had Mr. Bennet's consent, but that was several days too many.

Of course, some old-fashioned persons would say it was out of order to have asked the lady without her father's blessing. If she had been living in her own home, it would only have been a matter of a half-hour conversation, but the irregularity of the circumstances had lengthened what should have been a short interval.

He posted the letters without much ado.

As he pondered the problem, it did occur to him that a gentleman needn't get a father's blessing merely to show a preference for a lady. Darcy would not announce the engagement yet, but he could show his preference for Elizabeth. For to continue pretending indifference to her, as he had been doing for the last weeks since his disastrous first proposal, was distasteful to the point of nausea.

Lady Catherine would not like it, but perhaps it would be better to prepare her mind in such a way that the news of the engagement would not come as the shock it would otherwise.

On the way back to the hotel, satisfied in his mind as to the present course, he passed Chuff and Honoria again, and this time yielded to their entreaties to walk with them a pace.

Honoria leaned across her husband to look at him. "Your spirits took a decided turn for the better at the assembly."

"They did," Darcy agreed.

"I've rarely seen you stand up with so many young ladies."

"It's not my custom."

"Did you find any pleasing partners?"

"I did, in fact."

She sighed. "Darcy, you are a wretch and as unyielding as granite."

Chuff raised a hand. "Let be, my dear. Let be."

Her eyes twinkled. "My master has spoken. I shall keep my surmises to myself."

Mr. Darcy smiled. "As you always do exactly what you desire, I highly doubt that."

They continued their walk until they'd looped back to their own hotel, and Darcy took his leave.

Upon returning to the hotel, the ladies found that Mr. and Miss Bingley were on the point of departure, only staying to take their leave of Lady Catherine and her party.

This was soon done, but Lizzy could see that Miss Bingley was dissatisfied that Mr. Darcy was not yet returned.

"I will convey all that is proper to my nephew," Lady Catherine said regally. "There is no occasion for you to wait."

"I couldn't dream of dragging Charles away before he got to say goodbye to his friend. They may not see each other for months if he returns directly to Pemberley."

"Well, Caroline, I don't mind if— "

A quelling look from Caroline subdued her brother for a moment, but she seemed to realize she was being a bit obvious. With a gracious smile she turned to Georgiana and reminded her again to write to her. "Also, I want to invite you now, before the year slips away, to spend Christmas with us at Netherfield! I know Charles and Darcy would enjoy it enormously, and I would love to have the pleasure of your company! Wouldn't we, Charles? Do say they must come."

Georgiana smiled, but her words faltered. "Thank you, that is kind. I don't yet know— I am not the one who makes our plans—Christmas is so far away, isn't it?"

Lizzy couldn't help but think how Caroline would steam if she knew that by next Christmas, Lizzy herself would be the new Mrs. Darcy. It boggled the imagination, and Lizzy let out a sudden laugh.

Caroline narrowed her eyes.

Lizzy coughed. "Excuse me. Something diverting came to mind." She nodded to Georgiana. "It does seem impossible to think of Christmas in May! I can only think of summer. My aunt and uncle are taking a trip to the Lake District and have asked me to accompany them. Have you been there, Miss Darcy? Miss Bingley?"

This unexceptionable topic was canvassed briefly, though Lizzy was distracted when it occurred to her that perhaps she would not get to make the trip after all. Would Mr. Darcy want a short engagement? Or perhaps for her to spend some portion of the summer with his family? That would be perfectly normal, but she felt a pang at the thought of losing the treat with her Aunt and Uncle Gardiner.

Before the topic of the lakes was more than moderately wrung dry, Mr. Darcy returned.

The Christmas invitation was extended again, seconded by Charles, but Darcy refused to commit. He didn't quite refrain from looking at Lizzy, but he turned it into a sweeping look at the whole party. "I daresay we might make up a party at Pemberley this year, but I can hardly say as yet."

"At Pemberley? But you never do!" Miss Bingley exclaimed, pleased. "I would be delighted to come. I know Georgiana is not used to the role of hostess as yet, and I place all my experience at her disposal."

Georgiana looked as if she had been asked to set a broken bone. "A Christmas party? At Pemberley?"

Mr. Darcy's lips quivered. "Don't worry, my dear, I have a plan; I won't ask you to be the hostess."

There was a pause. Everyone's minds circled for a moment on the import of these words. A hostess there must be. Would he ask one of his aunts or was there a deeper meaning to his assurance? The results of their cogitations depended on their various personalities and interest in the question.

Miss Bingley turned pink.

Lizzy scarcely knew where to look. Did Mr. Darcy realize that he had inadvertently given Caroline hope?

After more goodbyes, two repetitions of delight at the Christmas idea, and one very ominous throat-clearing by Lady Catherine, the Bingleys departed. They were seen from the window to climb into their carriage and depart.

{ 24 }

I HAVE NO OPINION OF THAT woman," Lady Catherine said decidedly. "Very much the lady, I admit, but I wouldn't care to see her as mistress of Pemberley. Who are her parents, pray? Her connections? She places herself on a very high form."

Darcy didn't much care for his aunt's opinion, but he frowned. "Aunt, Charles is my particular friend and Caroline is his sister. Please don't disparage them."

Georgiana studied the carpet, and Colonel Fitzwilliam opened the newspaper.

Lady Catherine sniffed.

Darcy caught Elizabeth's eye and forgot about the conversation. *Elizabeth* at Pemberley for Christmas. What a pleasant thought.

Lady Catherine's thoughts were traveling the same direction, but not so happily. "If you do desire to have a party at Pemberley, I daresay I could make the trip. I haven't been to Pemberley in nigh on ten years. Of course, *I* would be willing to act as hostess, but if you'll be guided by me, the best solution is to have a wife by that time, but not the proud Miss Bingley. No one cares for an estate the way a true mistress does."

"Indeed—"

"Even Rosings, dare I say, had fallen into a shocking state before Sir Richard and I were wed. I managed everything, from the scouring of the wine cellar to the hiring of new household staff."

"I am certain you did everything that was needed."

Elizabeth's lower lip was tucked between her teeth as she went to sit in her favorite window seat. Was she on the verge of laughter or something else?

Lady Catherine settled back into her chair. "I see your expression, Darcy. You *are* thinking of Miss Bingley. I urge you to reconsider. She is fashionable, but that kind of fashion is only skin deep. She would turn Pemberley into one of these dreadfully modern showplaces. People of that sort have no sense of history."

Darcy did not relish the idea of fencing with his aunt in this manner for much longer. "Speaking of historical estates," he said, "I have heard that Penshurst, though sadly deteriorated, is well worth a visit. It's not much more than an hour ride. If my cousin is feeling well, perhaps we could visit today."

"Penshurst? Isn't it all but a ruin now?" Lady Catherine demanded.

"Not so bad as that, I hope. I was speaking with Sir John last spring, and he is considering restoration. He and his son are planning to retire there to begin overseeing the work personally."

This snatched Lady Catherine's interest, as Penshurst was one of the only other estates in the region of Rosings. She was in a frame of mind to wax eloquent on the inestimable value of your truly old English families and their historic properties.

Mr. Darcy, with what he knew to be contemptible duplicity, asked Georgiana if she would not enjoy riding with him the scant six miles to their destination? Georgiana's eyes lit up, as he expected they would.

"Yes, please," she said. "We've not ridden together for such a long time."

"Capital. Lady Catherine and Anne will take the carriage. Fitz, you will join us, yes? And perhaps Mrs. Annesley. How is she this morning?"

Georgiana's brow furrowed. "Much better, but in no case for riding. She could manage the carriage."

"Miss Bennet can accompany us, then," Darcy said. "And Mrs. Annesley in the carriage."

Lady Catherine, to his surprise, agreed at once. "Yes, of course, for Anne will ride with you as well, and Miss Bennet must needs accompany her."

Darcy was slightly taken aback. "But surely that will be too long a ride for my cousin. Twelve miles."

"Nonsense. She is much improved, and at Rosings she is often out of doors driving in her gig. The air and exercise will do her good."

Anne looked uncertain, but hopeful. "Riding is rather more demanding than driving, Mama. Though I admit it does seem a warm, pleasant day. And I do… I do feel rather stronger this week."

"Excellent!" Lady Catherine said triumphantly. "I congratulate myself on your improvement; it is marked."

"And if you do grow weary you may always return in the carriage," Darcy added.

"Yes, she will go," Lady Catherine said.

Darcy was just congratulating himself when Lizzy met his eyes apologetically. "Unfortunately, I do not have a riding habit with me; I am no great horsewoman."

Lady Catherine shrugged. "There is no need for a chaperone with a party composed entirely of family. Miss Bennet may ride in the carriage, and Mrs. Annesley may continue to convalesce."

Mr. Darcy's spirits sank. He probably ought to have guessed that Elizabeth did not have the proper attire—she was, as he well knew, fonder of walking than riding!—but it was not something that occurred to him. Georgiana did not ride often, but she would never go on a trip without a riding habit. When Elizabeth was his wife, he would make sure she had everything she needed.

But he was already trapped by his suggestion, so Darcy took himself off to the stables to inquire about hiring horses for Anne and Georgiana.

What with one thing and another, they left before the morning was over. Georgiana, at least, was still quite pleased at the unexpected treat, and even Anne seemed to be in better spirits. Perhaps the waters were doing her some good.

Darcy tried to shake off his sour mood.

Lizzy entered the chaise with Lady Catherine, none too pleased to have over an hour tête-à-tête with her. Perhaps the elder lady would sleep, as she had done on the way to the Wells.

She did not.

Her mind was still focused on the threat of Miss Bingley's "encroaching manners," and she enumerated the lady's many faults and failings to Lizzy for most of the drive. Lizzy alternated between a desire to laugh hysterically and a strange impulse to defend Miss Bingley. Lizzy did not think highly of Caroline; she regretted that Jane would probably have such a shallow, self-centered sister-in-law, but it was difficult to listen to Lady Catherine criticize anyone without a perverse desire to disagree.

Lizzy was relieved when they slowed at the gates of the estate they were to visit. Mr. Darcy came to hand them both out of the carriage and he pressed her fingers, with a slight smile.

To the left of the carriageway was a large sunken garden, which looked as if it had been laid out in grand symmetrical beds, but the hedges, grass, and trees were so overgrown they had all but obliterated the pathways. The central fountain was at present a slimy pool.

To their right lay the house, an imposing edifice of tan stone with battlements along the top and deep, narrow mullioned windows.

"We arrived half an hour ago," Darcy told Lizzy, "and have already made the acquaintance of the keeper and his wife. And we are in luck, my friend Sir John, the owner of Penshurst, is here visiting as well."

He spoke as if it was good news to introduce her to his friend, but didn't he realize that without revealing their engagement, his friend wouldn't look twice at her? Lizzy longed to know what he was thinking, but there was so little opportunity. She was somewhat reconciled to her last few days as a companion, but it was still irksome.

The house was at least three stories, with uneven but picturesque additions on both sides, including a round tower reaching above the rest, complete with spire. The stones were dark with wet around the edges, moss growing in the cracks. Several uneven stone buttresses flanked the oldest part of the building, along with stone tracery in the stained-glass windows.

"What a charming Gothic ruin," Lizzy said. "There is a tower for a queen and a hall-keep worthy of a knight. Or a knight's ghost."

Lady Catherine descended from the carriage with Mr. Darcy's help. "It is no such thing. Gothic, indeed. You got that from a novel."

"No, Miss Bennet is correct," Mr. Darcy said. "It was built in the fourteenth century and was heavily influenced by the Gothic architecture of the time."

"Thank you for the compliment," Lizzy said gaily, as the groom who'd driven the carriage began to lead away the horses, "but I did in fact 'get it' from a novel and was only accidentally correct. I know very little about such things. I have always struggled to pay attention to history for its own sake; I always cared more for the stories. And now that I am put in mind of it, did not Henry VIII meet his second wife, Anne, in such a place as this?"

"In this place, exactly," Lady Catherine answered proudly. "Her own home was at Hever Castle, also in Kent. It is an extremely historic district. Rosings is of a more recent date, but it is comparable to Hever in size and is its superior in comfort." Lady Catherine continued to reminisce as they made their way to the front door.

Corrie Garrett

Elizabeth took Mr. Darcy's offered arm and smiled up at him. Perhaps they could muddle through this first, awkward day of their engagement after all.

{ 25 }

S IR JOHN WAS FOUND TO BE IN a rear parlor, discussing politics with Colonel Fitzwilliam, while Georgiana and Anne sat on a dusty settee and sipped tea.

He seemed like an upright man, but hopelessly class-conscious. Whether the fault was Lizzy's air and attitude or Darcy's surreptitious attention to her, but the man seemed determined to snub her. After Lady Catherine introduced Lizzy as Miss de Bourgh's companion, it was as if Lizzy turned invisible. He barely gave her a nod.

When Lizzy kept joining the conversation, which she did before she had taken his measure and because the conversation was interesting, he grew grave and then rude. Several long looks and abrupt answers were followed by completely ignoring her interjections.

When Lady Catherine got to the point of requesting the tour they had come for, Sir John responded promptly. "Of course, my lady. You and your daughter and relatives of course." He summoned the lady who served them tea, the keeper's wife. "Hetty, would you make Miss de Bourgh's companion comfortable in your own parlor? She'll be fine there."

Lizzy's eyebrows winged upward, but it was nothing compared to the blush of mortification that spread over Mr. Darcy's cheeks.

"I know Miss Bennet is also eager to see the house," he said stiffly.

Sir John frowned but chose not to force the issue.

Lizzy considered excusing herself to allow the visit to pass more pleasantly, but... she *did* want to see everything. Anyway, she had always expected to be treated like this when she became a companion. It must have been the sheerest luck that she hadn't faced this sort of prejudice until now. She could certainly deal with it for another hour.

The tour was wonderful, though with the best will in the world not to exacerbate the man's temper, Lizzy still regularly forgot herself in enthusiasm and inquiry. Mr. Darcy, as they ascended the stairs from the hall keep to the wall walks behind the battlements, offered her his arm.

Lizzy was undeniably curious whether he would address the growing tension. Sir John's attitude was probably not far off what his own would have been if Mr. Darcy had met her under such circumstances. Would he acknowledge the continual slights? Ignore them? Fire up in her defense? The thought of a protective Mr. Darcy was appealing, but on the whole, she did not expect it. He might offer a slight apology or perhaps remind her that if Sir John knew her true circumstances he would never act so.

He pressed her hand instead and dipped his head low. "Shall we go at once? Would you prefer to leave?"

Lizzy was startled. That he would willingly curtail the visit, probably his only chance to speak to Sir John for months, was unexpected.

It was clearly a serious offer. His tone was soft, for her ears only, and his eyes promised that he would immediately carry out her wishes.

"And miss the tower rooms?" Elizabeth whispered. "Never." She gave him an understanding smile and he returned it gratefully.

He also retained her hand, resting gently on his arm. Lady Catherine was too distracted by the strong wind to notice. "No, this will not do." Her voice was nearly snatched away by the sharp wind. "Too much wind for me and far too much for Anne!"

Lizzy moved to follow them back into the door nestled behind the battlements, but Darcy stayed still, pressing her hand to wait. They lingered behind the others, even Georgiana disappearing down the stone stairs with a quick glance behind. The wind whipped at Lizzy's hair and bonnet and she put her free hand to it to keep it from being torn from her head.

The view from up here was exquisite. "The High Weald from on high," Lizzy said. "I love this." By which she meant all of it—the dramatic wind, the cloudy sky, the swept grayish-green plains and heathery purples of trees and shrubs, and—most of all—getting to share it with Mr. Darcy.

Mr. Darcy had lingered both to escape Sir John's stiff and unnecessary hauteur and to have a moment with Elizabeth. He turned to look at her. Her cheeks and lips were rosy with the high wind, her hair somewhat escaping the hat.

"I love it, too," he said.

Tentatively, giving her time to realize what he was doing, Mr. Darcy stooped to kiss her.

He wanted to touch her hair, her face, everything, but he settled for gripping her warm hands between his.

A particularly strong gust caused her to sidestep and he slid a hand up her arm, steadying her.

His forehead rested against hers. "I suppose we ought to follow lest someone come to retrieve us."

Lizzy nodded, not quite meeting his eyes. "I suppose so."

They followed the rest of the group down, making better time down the stairs than Lady Catherine and meeting their party at the bottom.

Darcy wanted to ask Elizabeth if she was glad or upset that he'd stolen a kiss, as they were engaged though not publicly. He wanted to ask if it was the revelation to her that it was to him.

But no, such an inquiry would be going too far. Kissing her was one thing, talking about it was somehow far more intimate.

Elizabeth was surprised when Mr. Darcy kept her with him the whole rest of the tour. There was time for Lady Catherine to notice. Georgiana, Anne, and the Colonel noticed as well.

Sir John looked increasingly disapproving and stiff, though that might have been the natural state of his face.

When they were in the gardens, Lady Catherine attempted to rearrange the grouping, but Mr. Darcy was uncharacteristically deaf to her suggestions. Colonel Fitzwilliam took over with a good grace and when Mr. Darcy steered her away from their companions, Elizabeth enjoyed the overgrown gardens prodigiously.

"I'm sure they'll be even more beautiful when they're tamed and trimmed," Elizabeth admitted, "but in general I don't love overly formal gardens. Don't you agree? Where nature is enhanced rather than being enslaved?"

Mr. Darcy gave her a strange look and Elizabeth flushed. "But of course, I have not seen Pemberley. Is it surrounded by formal gardens? It is, isn't it? Shall I wash my mouth out with soap?" she teased him, half-laughing, half-dismayed.

He shook his head. "The rose garden is the most formal, I suppose, but I think in general you will like the grounds. Derbyshire is a beautiful county, and my ancestors, thankfully, didn't see the need to change much. Enhanced, like you said, but not enslaved. There are trails for walking, indeed one that meanders ten miles around the home wood."

"Ten miles?" Elizabeth echoed. That was… large. "It sounds delightful. I haven't given much thought to Pemberley as yet."

"No, I know." He kicked a stray tendril of thorny vine out of their path. "Do you have any objection to riding? At Pemberley, I often ride. The distances to the tenants, the farms, and the neighbors make walking less eligible."

"No, no objection," Lizzy said at once, still trying to picture herself the mistress of an estate as large as what he implied. "It's never been much of an object for me, since the village is only a mile from Longbourn and our particular friends even closer. When I was learning to ride, I found our placid old horse too slow and declared it unconscionably dull."

"I'll look forward to finding you a horse that is not unconscionably dull, then."

When they all returned to the house, the carriage and horses were waiting. Mr. Darcy reluctantly released Lizzy.

Lady Catherine looked as if she'd eaten an unripe persimmon. Lizzy prepared herself for the devil of a ride. Alone in the carriage for an hour! Could she endure Lady Catherine's arrogant insults for so long without responding in kind? Lizzy was not good at remaining silent in the face of provocation, and she suspected she was about to receive a lot of provocation.

Mr. Darcy had turned away to say goodbye to Sir John and did not notice his aunt's ill-humor and Lizzy's dismay. Mr. Darcy was much less genial with his friend now. He was stiff and cold and barely deigned to shake the man's hand.

To Lizzy's immense relief, Anne approached the carriage, limping slightly. "I will accompany you, Mama. I am fatigued from walking, and I believe I turned my ankle on a loose stone."

Lady Catherine's eyes snapped. "If you'd been properly escorted, I'm sure it would have been avoided." Her glare laid the blame for this squarely at Lizzy's feet.

Anne did not reply but only took Colonel Fitzwilliam's hand as he helped her into the carriage.

The ride back to the hotel was silent. It was a tense, pregnant silence. Lady Catherine was angry. Anne was tired, but not tired enough to sleep. She leaned back in her corner with her eyes on the swaying ceiling.

When they alighted back at the hotel, Anne requested that Lizzy accompany her up to her room.

Lizzy followed Anne up the stairs but was so lost in thought, it was not until they reached Anne's room that she noted Anne's limp was gone. "Is your ankle feeling better? I hope so."

Lizzy shut the door behind them and went to stoke Anne's fire. Even Lizzy felt a bit chilled after being out most of the blustery day. When she turned back to Anne, Anne had an odd expression on her face.

It was… smug?

"You're welcome," Anne said. "Now we are even."

Lizzy wracked her brain. "We're even?"

"Yes." Anne sank down into the chair by the fire and began to remove her hat. "You drank the water for me that first day at the bath house, you recall? Now I spared you my mother's strictures on the ride home."

Lizzy would have been less surprised if Anne had thrown a piece of coal at her. "Your limp… you were help-ing *me*?"

Anne set aside the hat. Her lips pursed with distaste. "I did stumble on a stone, but it was not so bad. You were foolish to flirt with Mr. Darcy. My mother does not care if you flirt with the Colonel, but she does not like it when Darcy pays attention to other ladies."

"I was not *flirting,*" Lizzy protested.

Anne shrugged and leaned her head back. "As you will."

"You did not need to… repay me for the water," Lizzy added quietly. "I was trying to be your friend. Friends do kind things for each other without collecting debt."

"I do not believe our natures incline us to be friends, but thank you for the gesture." She sighed. "It is sometimes galling to always be the one in need. It was satisfying to have something to offer."

Lizzy wasn't sure how to feel. Normally she would think Anne's little deception with her mother was an overture of kindness, but it did not feel like that.

"Thank you," Lizzy said eventually. "I appreciate that you even noticed my predicament. For what it's worth, I think you have more to offer as a friend than you think you do."

"I don't need you any longer," Anne added. "You're free to go until dinner."

Lizzy shook her head and left the room quietly. She might never understand Anne de Bourgh.

{ 26 }

Darcy escorted Georgiana up to her room, leaving her at her door with a kiss on the cheek before going to his own room to change out of his riding clothes and dress for dinner.

He'd had a good ride with Georgiana and the Colonel, but he was still perturbed over how Sir John had treated Elizabeth. True, without all the information, he could not know the insult he had given to Darcy's future wife. However, shouldn't a gentleman be polite to a genteel young lady, even if she was a companion? Would he ever have acted thus?

He didn't think so but only because he would probably have paid very little attention to *any* of the women in such a group. He was too used to being considered a matrimonial prize, so he was largely silent with women he did not know well.

Concerned with Sir John's behavior, Darcy did not considered his aunt's mood until he regained the parlor before dinner and found her berating Elizabeth.

They were the only two in the room. Lady Catherine had not even gone up to change her dress, but still wore the slightly dusty gown she'd worn to Penshurst. Darcy saw and felt the thump as she smacked her cane hard into the plush carpet.

"—and you still have the effrontery to throw out lures to my nephew. Right in front of my eyes. I believed that you had more decorum; more respect for my family. Instead, I see that you have repaid my forbearance by redoubling your efforts. I can only believe that you deliberately lied when you told me—"

Mr. Darcy cleared his throat, throttling back his intense anger. "I think you are under a misapprehension, ma'am." He took Elizabeth's hand. "I have asked Miss Elizabeth to marry me, and she graciously accepted. Through we await her father's approval, we are affianced, and I will thank you to speak to her as the future Mrs. Darcy."

If he'd thought Lady Catherine would be silenced, he was wrong.

"Her father's approval? What of *my* approval? What of Anne? This is *nonsense.*"

Darcy's jaw was clamped so hard his teeth ached. "The nonsense is your continual and unfounded assumption that I will offer for Anne. I have nothing but regard for my cousin, but she is not going to be my wife. I am sorry if that pains you, but it is my decision."

"*Her*, mistress of Pemberley?" Lady Catherine looked witheringly at Elizabeth. "*Her*—"

Footsteps approached the parlor causing her to break off with an angry gasp.

"Excuse me, miss," one of the hotel footmen said to Elizabeth, "but there is a family downstairs as says they would like to see you."

"A—a family?"

"A Mr. and Mrs. Bennet, and daughters."

Elizabeth's body grew stiff next to him. "Oh my."

Elizabeth turned to Mr. Darcy with blankest astonishment. "I – I suppose I'll go down to see them. Our letters…?"

"Have not had time to arrive," Mr. Darcy said, "as they were only posted this morning."

"Of course." She dropped a slight, distracted curtsey to Lady Catherine and followed the footman down to the front, common parlor.

If she'd thought Lady Catherine's tirade had filled the cup of the day's unexpected problems, it was as nothing to how she felt now.

She entered the room and Kitty threw herself on Lizzy. "Here we are!" she crowed. Jane stood near the window with her hands clasped, looking unhappy and ashamed, her normal serenity clearly lacking. Mary studied the books in the elegant bookshelf between the windows, sniffing in contempt. Lizzy's father reclined in a large chair by the fire, with a newspaper open, looking as unconcerned as if he were alone at a club. And Lizzy's mother bounced up from the chaise lounge, demanding to know "whether Mr. Bingley and his sister were at this hotel or another?"

Kitty was talking in her other ear. "It was so unfair that Lydia got to go to Brighton without me, but Mama says I may perhaps visit if Jane makes haste with Mr. Bingley. She even says that I may buy a new dress in London!"

Kitty's ringlets were tangled and messy, and Lizzy automatically smoothed them with her hand while Kitty exclaimed, "It is only fair that I get a new dress and not Lydia, for I am the shortest and none of Jane or Mary's gowns fit me."

"But you did not answer me," Mrs. Bennet repeated, "are Mr. and Miss Bingley situated here or at a different hostelry?" She lowered her voice. "No disrespect to Lady Catherine, but I want to know before we take rooms here."

"I don't even know if there are rooms to be had," Lizzy said. She was devoutly thankful this room was currently empty except for her family. "But the Bingleys left this morning for London, so—"

"Oh no!" Mrs. Bennet wailed. "We are too late. It is most unfortunate. I told you, Mr. Bennet, that we should have come at once, but you *would* wait. The waters will do wonders for my nerves, I said, but you did not care."

"I daresay the waters are still here, my dear," he said, turning a page. He gave Lizzy a fond smile, a twinkle in his eye. Lizzy tried not to be hurt that he had not truly greeted her yet.

"Much good that will do me!"

Jane had recovered her color and breathed a sigh of relief. "Then they are not here."

Disentangling herself from her younger sister, Lizzy went to Jane and embraced her.

"I could not dissuade Mother," Jane murmured apologetically. "Mr. Collins mentioned in a letter that Mr. Bingley was here as well, and she became determined to bring the family. She wanted very much to go to Brighton, but when that did not happen, she settled on Tunbridge."

Lizzy winced. She had written about the Bingleys to Charlotte, and of course Mr. Collins would learn of their presence here.

"I'm sure it's been years since we had a proper holiday," Mrs. Bennet argued with Jane. "Why should we not come? Longbourn is dull and quiet these days."

"Is it though?" Mr. Bennet asked ironically.

"But now I don't know what to do," Mrs. Bennet said. "It is the greatest mischance."

"We should go back to London," Kitty offered at once. "Bingley is there and so are the shops and millineries! Why stay in this stupid place?"

On those words, Mr. Darcy appeared in the doorway.

Mrs. Bennet looked to see who it was, but her countenance fell obviously when she encountered him. With barely a "Mr. Darcy," in his direction, she turned to her husband. "How long would it take to return to my brother Gardiner's?"

"Quite a while, considering I have paid and sent off the post boys. You would be required to walk, though I daresay your determination would give you strength." He didn't even look up from his paper.

Lizzy wished she might fall into the earth.

Mr. Darcy came to Elizabeth's side. "Good evening, Mrs. Bennet. Mr. Bennet."

Thus roused from his paper, Mr. Bennet rose and greeted Mr. Darcy but clearly his mind was otherwhere. "Mr. Darcy, of course. Excuse me, I shall go see if we shall find rooms or find ourselves in the hedgerows."

"Could I have a word with you first?" Mr. Darcy asked. "Perhaps in the taproom?"

Lizzy felt as if she had drunk a particularly strong cordial. Would he ask her father for her hand *now*? It seemed an inauspicious moment, but Darcy was already exiting the room with her father, who looked slightly curious but in no way concerned. Of course, Mr. Darcy had just informed

Lady Catherine of their engagement, so there could be no waiting. Lizzy pinched the bridge of her nose.

She hadn't told Darcy about her father's bad investment either. Should she already have broached her lack of dowry?

"Whatever could *he* have to say to your father?" Mrs. Bennet demanded. "I see that Mr. Darcy is still as proud and unpleasant as before, though I daresay it was good of him to come down and greet us. I don't know why he should trouble himself, however; it is not as though he ever pretended to be friendly in Hertfordshire. We are certainly not here to see *him*."

"Hush, Mama," Lizzy said helplessly. "He might hear you."

"So what if he hears me? He didn't scruple to disparage you when you could hear him."

"That was so long ago—"

"Well, I'm sure I don't care any longer. It was Mr. Bingley I was hopeful to see here, and he is gone! There has been some great misunderstanding in this. I have told Jane there must be some misunderstanding. I refuse to believe Mr. Bingley had not real intentions."

"Please don't, Mama," Jane said tiredly. "Lizzy, are you well? You are very flushed."

"I'm fine." She was not fine. She could not imagine how her father was taking this news. And when they were done talking, they would come back. The announcement would be made!

She'd hoped that when her mother learned of Mr. Darcy's offer, he would not be nearby. Preferably in a different country! The revelation was sure to involve all of them in embarrassment.

She simply must prepare her mother. Lizzy raised her chin. "I believe I know why Mr. Darcy is talking to my father. He… has asked me to marry him, and I accepted."

Jane's lovely eyes went quite comically wide. Kitty's mouth hung open like a fish. Mary turned from the books with a frown, and her mother pressed a palpitating hand to her bosom. "You… accepted him?"

"Yes." There was much to explain there, but she could not pour out her heart to her mother. They had never had that kind of relationship, nor would Kitty or even Mary be discreet. In the plainest terms, she described how she had become better acquainted with him in the last months and believed that his previous pride was misunderstood. "In short, on knowing him better, I believe that we shall be very happy together."

"Happy?" echoed Kitty. "But Mr. Darcy is so proud and disagreeable and not even so very handsome. He insulted you! Do you truly think you ought to marry him? I'm sure I should never marry any but an officer who loved me."

Lizzy smiled wryly. "You may find that eventually the officer part of that dream is unnecessary. But as to whether

I ought to marry Mr. Darcy, well, I have given my word, and as I like him better than any other gentleman of my acquaintance, I have no desire to draw back."

Jane looked grave. She came and put her hand gently on Lizzy's shoulder. "You would not... I think Father perhaps overstated his losses in his letter. But I know you would not sacrifice yourself for monetary reasons. Therefore... I must wish you happy."

"Thank you, Jane." Quietly, Lizzy added, "Perhaps tonight I can explain more fully."

"Ten thousand a year," breathed Mrs. Bennet.

Lizzy grimaced. This was what she dreaded. "Yes, Mama. But he very much does not like to speak of wealth or—or finances."

"Why not?" asked Kitty.

"Of course not," Mrs. Bennet agreed. "It would be vulgar to appear overly conscious of his wealth. But Lizzy! You will be beyond anything great! Mr. Bingley is nothing to it. Oh, I am so glad we've come!"

Lizzy was less glad, but when she had a moment to reflect, she thought perhaps it was for the best. Now that Lady Catherine knew of the engagement, Lizzy would need to leave. She could travel home with her family, hopefully starting tomorrow.

She also wanted desperately to tell Jane that Bingley was on his way back to London to see *her,* but there was no opportunity in the midst of her mother's raptures and Kitty's forthright questions.

Into the midst of this familial chaos, Mr. Bennet came to the door and motioned for Lizzy to come out to him.

He escorted her into the empty taproom; Mr. Darcy was nowhere to be seen.

"He has gone up to apprise Lady Catherine of our arrival. Ah, and I think he means to bring his sister down to meet us."

He sat heavily on a stool and looked at Lizzy. "What have you done, Lizzy? Why would you accept a man you dislike so cordially?"

"You did not… refuse him?" Lizzy asked.

"No, but I nearly called him a liar." He laughed at her suddenly blanched face. "I did not, my dear. But I was shocked."

"I wrote to you, but the letter is still on its way to Longbourn."

"Is this an elaborate ruse to teach me a lesson? I won't deny you have cause to be disillusioned with me. If that is the case, consider me chastened and end your play here."

"Papa, I'm not trying to punish you at all."

"I won't say I don't deserve it, but I should hate to see you suffer a lifetime for my mistakes."

"Papa!"

"No, I know you would not be that kind of fool."

"I am not any kind of fool, I hope," Lizzy said, a little sharply. She took a deep breath and explained more of the circumstances to her father, particularly concerning Mr. Wickham. "As for Mr. Darcy's character, I believe seeing him amongst his family, particularly his love for his sister, has allowed me to know him far better."

"But do you love him? Do you respect him?" her father asked. "You have always said you would not marry without love, and I could not bear to see you marry without respect."

"I do not know if I love him quite yet," Lizzy admitted slowly, "but I do respect him, and I do feel something I believe must approach love."

"Well, he certainly seems determined on you. He did not even blink when I told him of my faulty investment last fall. Said all that he ought of his disinterest and love. If I could be sure of *your* happiness, I would feel easy."

"You may be easy. I *am* happy." Lizzy would have given more reassurances, but a brief knock brought them both back to the doorway where Mr. Darcy stood with Georgiana on his arm.

.

HE HAS TOLD ME THE GOOD NEWS," Georgiana
said eagerly. "I am so happy."

Her arms twitched as if she would hug Lizzy,
but she held back, smiling uncertainly.

"As am I!" Lizzy exclaimed, embracing her.

Georgiana clung quite tightly for a moment. Her eyes
were suspiciously bright when she pulled away. She turned
to Darcy, "Was this what you meant about Christmas? That
Lizzy would be with us?"

"Yes, that is what I had in mind." He smiled at Lizzy,
and they shared a brief moment of joy and camaraderie in
the midst of this crazy evening. She knew she would remember that look for a long time.

Georgiana broke the silence. "And this is your father?"

Recalled to her duties, Lizzy performed the introduction
before escorting Georgiana to meet her mother and sisters.

A truly horrific sight met their eyes. Lady Catherine stood in the midst of the Bennets. She was planted like a statue of outrage and seemed to be demanding that they leave.

Lizzy's mother, to do her credit, was trying to be placating. "To be sure, I did not mean to surprise your ladyship. If Lizzy kept this a secret, the naughty girl, I daresay you have had quite the shock. Do sit down." She patted a cushion as she spoke.

"A secret? I should say so. A secret engagement. Her family coming for an engagement party without so much as a by your leave. Fine doings among the riffraff, but—"

Kitty and Mary both looked on in shock.

Jane wrung her hands. "You misunderstand, ma'am, we had no more idea of the engagement than you did."

But Lady Catherine didn't hear Jane's soft voice. "I did your daughter a *favor*, and this is how I am repaid?"

Mrs. Bennet patted the cushion again. "I'm certain Lizzy is ever so grateful. If we are to be family—"

"Family! Are the halls of Pemberley to be thus polluted? You will remove yourselves at once."

Mr. Darcy dropped Georgiana's arm and advanced into the room. "Aunt, what is the meaning of this? Elizabeth's family have every right to be here. You are overwrought. Allow me to escort you back to your rooms."

"Overwrought!" She thumped the floor with her cane. "I am in perfect control of my faculties."

Mr. Darcy took her arm, steering her inexorably toward the door. "Then you will see that it is most improper to have this conversation in a public room. Anything you need to say *to me* you may say in the privacy of your suite."

He had not got her entirely out of the room when a commotion in the hall drew everyone's attention.

Kitty slipped around Darcy and his aunt and stuck her head into the hall. She pulled back and announced with glee, "It is Mr. Bingley!"

Darcy felt a dull headache forming behind his eyes. "It cannot be Mr. Bingley; he would have been home hours ago."

But he was wrong, as he saw when he and Lady Catherine took a few more steps and came in sight of the large door that led from the side yard. It *was* Mr. Bingley, and a cross, tired, mud-splattered Caroline.

"That woman again," Lady Catherine said harshly. "I suppose it no longer matters, but I still do not like her."

Caroline did not appear to hear this. "Charles, tell them to make up our rooms again, on the instant. My feet are ice."

The proprietor of the hotel gestured vaguely in the direction of Mr. Bennet. "I am so sorry, but the last three rooms, including yours, were just given to this gentleman."

"What? Already?" Caroline demanded. "Is it not enough that we should have a carriage accident? And that we should not see a helpful soul for hours?" Then she took in the people now crowding the hall around them, and her mouth moved soundlessly as she processed the arrival of the Bennets.

Mr. Darcy's eyes traveled from his aunt to Elizabeth's family to Caroline. His sister stood off to one side with Colonel Fitzwilliam, Georgiana looking bewildered and Fitz amused.

To be sure, he had wanted to shorten the days before he could announce his engagement to Elizabeth, but this was ridiculous.

Elizabeth pressed a hand to her mouth, but when she removed it, he saw that she was on the verge of laughter, not tears. "This is… too much." She laughed helplessly. "It's all too dreadful."

Darcy felt his own lips twitch.

Lady Catherine shook Mr. Darcy's arm. "How long do you intend to keep me standing in this very chill hall?"

"Not long at all. Let me escort you back to your room."

"But what of me?" Caroline asked. "I demand that we be given back our rooms. We've only been gone a matter of hours."

"Come, Caroline," Charles said. "If necessary, we will walk over to one of the hotels across the square."

"I refuse to walk another foot. I am *exhausted*."

The proprietor looked desperately at Mr. Darcy.

Kitty had edged around to get a better view of the commotion. "What happened? Did you have to walk all the way here? Lawd, how unlucky you are! First Mr. Darcy and now this."

Caroline ignored her. "Charles, you must be firm…"

She trailed off as she realized that her brother had abandoned her. Bingley had seen Jane and was, as far as Darcy could tell, no longer aware of anyone else.

Realizing it was incumbent on him to take charge, Mr. Darcy turned to Mr. Bennet. "Would you and your family be willing to stay at the Warwick? I would be happy to discharge the cost for your trouble." He added in an undertone, "It may be as well to have some space."

"Space!" Lady Catherine grumbled.

Mr. Bennet eyed him approvingly. "Quite. Come along, girls," he said to Kitty and Mary and Jane.

Caroline was looking on with confusion and disapproval, particularly at Bingley and Jane.

They both seemed to be tongue-tied, and Darcy did not have much patience for it tonight. Then he spotted Colonel Fitzwilliam, still lurking near the stairs with an amused smirk.

Darcy jerked his head at him. "Lady Catherine is tired and cold, please escort her back up while I settle things here."

Relieved of that burden, he turned to see that Jane at least had found her voice.

"I believe we are going." Jane curtseyed to Mr. Bingley. "I am quite… I am happy to have seen you again. Good evening."

Bingley pressed her hand. "I was looking forward to calling on you tomorrow, in London. Providence must have sent us back because you are here."

Jane blushed and her serene face gave way to a flickering, hopeful smile. If Darcy had wanted proof that her heart was engaged, he had it.

"Oh—" she said.

"Jane," called Mr. Bennet.

"May I call on you tomorrow?" Bingley asked.

Darcy turned to Elizabeth, who was no longer laughing, but looking with great satisfaction on Jane's farewell to his friend.

"Ought I to make myself scarce as well?" Elizabeth asked with a twinkle in her eye. "You've certainly borne enough tonight."

"No," Darcy said. "I need to speak with you before you retire." Perhaps *need* was too strong a word. There was no item of business that could not wait for tomorrow, but he selfishly wanted to talk to her again tonight after this brouhaha.

Georgiana melted away up the stairs, leaving only Caroline and Bingley with them.

Lizzy couldn't help but smile at Bingley's glowing mood, so opposite to his sister's sour face. He seemed completely oblivious to her anger. He shook Elizabeth's hand warmly. "Your family is here, I see. What a pleasant treat for you."

"Yes, quite," Lizzy agreed, laughingly. "They surprised me."

"Yes, I thought they must have. You would have told me if... And it has all worked out for the best! Good-natured of your parents to leave the rooms for us, also."

Mr. Bingley's powers of being pleased were in full force. He could find fault with no person or circumstance tonight. "Our carriage wheel struck a rock hidden in the weeds on the side of the road. Unfortunately it was at just such an angle as to crunch a spoke and wrench it out of alignment. And it was not my driving, Darcy! You know how these things happen! But it could have been much worse. An easy fix, and thankfully it happened during the day when we had plenty of time to walk."

Caroline looked as if she could have boxed her brother's ears. "Could have been much worse? I was certain we need only wait for someone to come along the road and render us assistance. But we waited for hours and no one came!"

Bingley shrugged. "I did tell you at the outset that the Mail had already passed by, and that the London-Tunbridge road is not heavily traveled at this time of year."

"Did you walk the whole way back?" Darcy asked, somewhat appalled.

"No, not at all," Bingley said cheerfully. "We were taken up by a farm cart before we'd gone more than three miles."

"Three *miles*," Miss Bingley repeated heatedly.

Lizzy met Darcy's eyes, saw the smile lurking there. "That is indeed too far," Lizzie agreed.

"Yes, it is," Caroline said shortly. She looked from Lizzy to Darcy and back again. "Is there… Is something…"

Mr. Darcy brought Lizzy's hand under his arm to link them. "You may both wish me happy. I am pleased to say that Miss Elizabeth and I are engaged."

"Engaged?" she repeated, somewhat piteously. "*Engaged?*"

"It is quite recent," he said, "and it was private until I could speak with her father. I shall of course send an announcement to the *Gazette*, though if tonight continues at its current pace it will be unnecessary, as everyone will already know."

Lizzy choked back a laugh.

Caroline Bingley, to give her her due, knew how to conduct herself like a lady. Her aching feet were forgotten, her shattered hopes set aside. She rose to the occasion and said all that was proper in such circumstances. Truly she behaved better than she had only moments before; the shock seemingly erased all smaller considerations from her head.

"Please excuse me," she said after a moment. "I shall retire."

When Charles also went up to change out of his muddy clothes in his former room, Mr. Darcy and Lizzy were finally alone. Alone that is, apart from the hotel staff who bustled about, bringing up the Bingleys' bags now retrieved from their carriage, and answering other summonses.

Lizzy pressed a hand to her eyes. "That could all have gone better."

She peeked at Mr. Darcy and found him looking grave.

"I do wish my family had not arrived at such an inopportune moment," Lizzy offered, trying to look on the bright side. "But it is not so bad. You were able to speak to my father, and now I may travel home with no inconvenience to you…"

"I am not silent because I am angry," Mr. Darcy said, "not angry with you, at any rate. I am mortified that my aunt insulted and belittled you, and indeed your whole family. I have rarely been more shocked."

Lizzy opened her mouth to say something a little impertinent about how un-shocked *she* was, but she realized that he was not ready to make light of the situation.

"It was not well done," Lizzy agreed, "but I won't regard it any longer if you won't. You were right, Lady Catherine *was* overwrought. She is used to getting her own way;

she is not accustomed to being presented with a *fait accompli.*"

Lizzy stepped forward to allow a kitchen maid with a tray of food to pass by. "I suppose I ought to discreetly retire soon, but I admit I am ravenous. Perhaps you could ask them to bring a little dinner to my room."

Darcy nodded but still looked uncharacteristically lost.

Tentatively, Lizzy put her hand on his arm. "It truly will be fine," she said again. "My mama, though she has her faults, will not hold a grudge, and my father is likely to laugh at the whole evening. We have established that I am fine, therefore there is nothing left to settle. You are probably feeling the lack of your own dinner and will be the better for it."

Mr. Darcy looked at her hand on his arm, and then tucked it under his own, turning them towards the large door that led out of the hotel. "I cannot and will not go up and eat with Lady Catherine at this moment, I would not be answerable for the consequences."

"But—but where are we going?" Lizzy asked as he led her out.

"We are going... to dine with Chuff and Honoria."

"But they don't expect us... And walking out alone..."

"We *are* officially engaged now."

"True, but I do not think walking in the dark is considered quite the thing." Lizzy laughed as he led her across the square. It was just now twilight, and the lamps were not lit.

"The dark in Tunbridge Wells is less improper than the dark in London," Mr. Darcy explained.

"Are you teasing me?"

"You don't have a shawl or coat, are you too cold?" he asked instead.

"No, I'm quite warm. I am merely startled. I have never thought you impetuous."

Mr. Darcy shook his head and laughed. "No, that I have not been. If I were impetuous, I would have asked you to marry me before we left Netherfield. Or at Hunsford, when I took such care to walk with you every morning."

"Did you? I thought you were intolerably bored."

"No, but my life *before* you was certainly boring."

"Well, on the authority of Lady Catherine, I am said to be a lively companion."

As the stars began to appear in the darkening sky, Mr. Darcy kissed her for the second time. "That you are," he agreed. "And now you are *my* lively companion."

.

Epilogue

THE NEXT MORNING LIZZY removed from the Holbourne Hotel to join her family at the War-wick.

She did not see Lady Catherine, but she did bid the others goodbye. Georgiana was in Mrs. Annesley's room, and Lizzy was glad to see the older lady was almost completely restored.

Lizzy shook her hand warmly. "You have been most kind to me these last few weeks. I look forward to seeing you again soon."

Lizzy had wondered if Mrs. Annesley would be disapproving when she learned of the engagement, but Lizzy ought to have known better. Mrs. Annesley was too well-bred. She took Lizzy's hand with a little stiffness but no observable condemnation. "I wish you happy, Miss Bennet. Miss Darcy has been telling me all. I daresay you thought me rather meddling these past weeks, but I did not realize what was in the wind."

Lizzy laughed. "How could you, when I did not either? And now I am afraid it is my turn to ask a favor. Miss de Bourgh is without a companion, as Lady Catherine does not want me to…continue with them. I'm going to return to London with my family. If you would be so kind as to render Miss de Bourgh any assistance in the next few days, I would thank you."

The goodbye with Anne was rather colder and the separation likely to be of a longer duration.

Lizzy also felt a little sorry for her. She wasn't sure to what extent Anne had expected to be Mr. Darcy's wife, but Lizzy could not very well ask such a bold question.

"Farewell," Lizzy said instead. "I understand that Mrs. Jenkinson will be returning soon. I wish you all the best."

Anne's face was impossible to read. "Goodbye, Miss Bennet. I do not think Mama and I will be attending the wedding, but I… wish you well."

"Please give my love to Charlotte," Lizzy added.

"I will."

At the Warwick with her family, everything was a bit chaotic, as normal, but not as loud and boisterous as it would have been were Lydia present.

Mr. Darcy and Mr. Bingley escorted her there, with a porter behind bringing her parcels and chest of clothing.

Mrs. Bennet was all attention to Mr. Darcy, offering him breakfast, coffee, and all the best chairs as soon as he entered.

"Thank you, I've already eaten," he said. "I thought perhaps we might discuss the wedding."

"Oh yes, of all things!" Mrs. Bennet agreed. "Lizzy will never think of everything she ought. The bride clothes! The trousseau! The wedding carriage….!"

Lizzy winced. "I *will* think of it, Mama, as needed. But I believe Mr. Darcy is speaking more of what date we shall choose, and… and so on."

It was an awkward, embarrassing conversation. Her mother was trying to be considerate, clearly, but she could not help but be a little vulgar. She could not tear her mind away from Mr. Darcy's wealth.

In the end, they decided on a date in late July, when Lizzy's Aunt and Uncle Gardiner would be back from their summer tour. It hurt Lizzy a little to realize that she would not get to travel with them; indeed, that she would never travel with them in that way again. But she comforted herself with the thought of being able to host them at Pemberley, though with a side glance at Mr. Darcy's stoic face, she did not suggest it just then.

He was also trying to be affable, but he could not be quite the same person with her mother that he was with her. Perhaps that was true of every man!

Jane and Mr. Bingley were situated a little apart, near the empty fireplace, and if Jane's smiles were any indication, they had both overcome their unfortunate separation.

When Lizzy was afraid that Darcy could take no more of her mother and Kitty's interjections on ribbon, flowers, and wedding breakfasts, she spoke up, "Could we not take one more turn about the Upper Walk before leaving? Jane will adore it."

"Oh yes, my dear, of all things. All you young people should go. Take a shawl, Kitty, you have been sniffling this past hour."

Jane and Bingley led the way with Lizzy and Darcy just behind. Kitty and Mary brought up the rear.

By the time they had returned, Jane's eyes were shining. Mr. Bingley awkwardly asked to speak to Mr. Bennet privately.

"The next time I travel, I shall take a suite," he grumbled. "Thereby to have an office wherein to receive all the young men who have urgent need to speak with me." But he looked pleased nonetheless.

Mrs. Bennet wrung her hands with joy. "I just knew that Jane must come to Tunbridge Wells. Did I not say it, Kitty? Did I not, Mary? You have such a good father, girls, to go to such lengths for you."

Kitty wiped her nose with a handkerchief. "And the best of it is that Lydia did not get to see *any* of it! I shall have ever so much to tell her, and that will pay her back for gloating about Brighton."

"Brighton?" Mr. Darcy asked.

As her mother launched into an explanation of Lydia's "good fortune," Lizzy winced. It was going to be a long summer.

The End

Corrie Garrett

Thank you for reading!
Continue with *A True Likeness,*
Book 2 of the Austen Ensemble series!

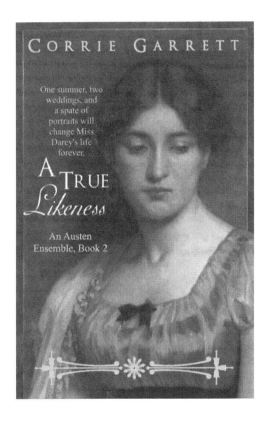

L IZZY AND DARCY HAVE reached an understanding and their short-lived secret is out. However, Lydia, Wickham, and even Georgiana will ensure that the summer has its fair share of catastrophes and surprises!

Join Lizzy, Darcy, and Georgiana as they navigate the dangerous waters of identity, family, and compromise.

Sneak Peak: Chapter 1

*D*EAR GEORGIANA,

    Your brother insists on calling me Elizabeth rather than Lizzy. I do not at all mind, but has he always struggled with nicknames? Were you ever Georgie or Anna or some other pet name?

    I am trying to gauge the depth of his formality, you see, the scope of the excavation I have taken on. Sometimes I do not know how to go on with him! It is rather like using the finest china every day. How does one relax?

    It is very formidable to be always Elizabeth, and the soon-to-be Elizabeth Darcy is even more austere. I am not at all sure that Elizabeth Darcy would be impertinent or unconventional, which Lizzy too often is!

    But enough of that, you asked after my sisters, and I can only say that they are well, but each is well according to her nature. Jane is in such transports of happiness that were our entire home to be washed away in a flood—it is such a rainy summer!—she would find something good to say of it.

    Mary has discovered a new interest in a book of Christian martyrs and is always ready with a cheerful anecdote of dismemberment or raging beasts when we run out of top-ics during our wedding visits.

And Kitty is at last reconciled to staying home this sum-mer because of the wedding. She has even ceased to long for Brighton and the officers more than once a day. My youngest sister, Lydia, is still visiting there, you see, and that has been a sad blow to Kitty's fortitude.

Jane and I have decided on a joint wedding day, with Mr. Bingley's and your brother's approval. I don't think my mother loves the idea of forgoing two wedding feasts for one, but we brought her around by pointing out that the novelty would make it the talk of Hertfordshire for at least a twelvemonth.

And how are you faring at Rosings? I am still full of admiration and a certain amount of guilt that you have thrown yourself into the breach. It was incredibly kind of you to have compassion on Lady Catherine. Remember that reinforcements are but a letter away, should you change your mind. Merely ask and we will be there directly!

Yours,

Lizzy

Georgiana tiptoed quietly into the library, where her cousin Anne was sitting for a portrait. The thick floral car-pet helped muffle her footsteps, but still somehow the por-traitist, Mr. Turner, sensed her approach, throwing a quick look and greeting in her direction.

"Good afternoon, Miss Darcy."

His easel was set up about three yards from Anne's position, which was just next to the glass doors of the terrace.

The heavy mahogany desk which had formerly occupied that spot had been removed by three footmen and the butler to the other side of the library, where it blocked at least four tiers of shelved books.

In its place had been put a graceful chintz lounge, Anne's seat for the portrait.

Heavy, spattered drop cloths protected the area around the easel, and a strong smell of turpentine and oil pervaded the room.

On the wall behind Anne's position was the de Bourgh coat of arms, carefully positioned for the portrait. Through the doors could be seen the low, graceful pillars that surrounded the terrace, a bit of the fields beyond, and the sky.

Today it was cloudy and gray, a dark day for June, but in the painting, diffuse sunlight seemed to spill into the room both from the door and from the viewer's left side. It was not quite the moody lighting of the romantics, but Georgiana secretly thought it was beautiful.

Mrs. Annesley, Georgiana's own companion, crocheted near the fireplace, which was lit for warmth. Georgiana drifted toward her and warmed her cold hands by the fire.

Today Mr. Turner would continue putting Anne into the beautifully painted background.

For the moment, he had set the canvas aside and was sketching Anne's face on paper.

Anne was well-dressed, but her face held very little expression.

"It looks as if we might have a summer shower today," Mr. Turner said. "Will you drive out as usual, Miss de Bourgh?"

"Yes."

He began to darken the fold line above Anne's right eye, and Georgiana was drawn forward almost against her will. She didn't want to be a bother or a distraction, but she did find it so interesting to watch him draw.

"What do you think about when you drive?" he asked.

"I have never considered."

Mr. Turner's hand hesitated for the briefest moment around her mouth, but then he kept refining the sketch. "Do you prefer to take the same route every day, or do you enjoy variation?"

"Generally, the same. I drive by the parsonage and speak with Mr. or Mrs. Collins if they are at home. I circle to the north, around the village, and then back to Rosings." She said all this in a near monotone.

Mr. Turner's straight shoulders slumped slightly. "Thank you, Miss de Bourgh, that will be all for today. I have the positional sketch, but with the light so poor, I cannot do much more. Thank you for your time."

She rose and curtseyed properly. "Until dinner, Mr. Turner."

Mrs. Annesley began to pack up her yarn, and Mr. Turner, his pencils. He was a man of medium height, sturdy but not much taller than Georgiana herself, and always dressed plainly, in dark colors.

"Were you trying to make her smile?" Georgiana asked.

He looked around at her. He was not handsome in the established way, but had a square, honest face, blue eyes, and thick hair between sand and brown that he kept unfashionably short.

"Not necessarily smile," he said carefully. "The goal is to find something that brings out her personality, a look to capture, an intensity, but… She is very self-controlled."

Georgiana knew exactly what he meant. He didn't want to paint her cousin looking pale and lifeless, but unfortunately that was often how Anne de Bourgh looked in real life.

"The only time I have seen her look quite happy was at the Ashford Races," Georgiana offered. "She likes horses."

"Perhaps I could set up my easel there." He smiled ruefully. "But I doubt your aunt would approve."

#

Will he get his chance? Find out in *A True Likeness...*

Author's Note

THANKS FOR READING! As a lover of all things Austen and a voracious reader of JAFF (Jane Austen fan-fiction), I appreciate you taking the time to immerse yourself in my story!

Who am I? I'm an indie writer and homeschool mom in Southern California. I enjoy writing both romance and science fiction with romance, humor, and happy endings.

If you need more to read after An Austen Ensemble, you might also enjoy my Emma and Pride and Prejudice series *From Highbury with Love.*

Thanks again for joining me!

Corrie Garrett

Find me on Facebook at Corrie Garrett, Author
Or on my website: www.corriegarrett.com

Made in the USA
Middletown, DE
23 April 2023

29339166R00158